shooting Elvis

'Eversz's novel reads like *The Catcher in the Rye*
with high explosives'
Daily Telegraph

'A thriller with complex characterisation, a streak
of misanthropic wit, a bleak world-weariness, and no
easy answers . . . *Shooting Elvis* is that rare creature, a
Generation X novel that skips the lifestyle accessories
and goes to the heart of the malaise'
The Scotsman

'Good fun'
The Times

'Pulp fiction fun amok'
Time Out

'A groovy little debut, and no mistake'
Melody Maker

'Wild, wicked and off the wall . . .
Fast,

D1350093

R. M. Eversz lived in Los Angeles for more than a decade, working as a film-maker and screenwriter, and currently resides in Prague.

R. M. Eversz

shooting Elvis

Confessions of an Accidental Terrorist

PAN BOOKS

First published in the United States of America 1996 by Grove Press

First published in the United Kingdom 1996 by Macmillan

This edition published 1997 by Pan Books
an imprint of Macmillan Publishers Ltd
25 Eccleston Place, London SW1W 9NF
and Basingstoke

Associated companies throughout the world

ISBN 0 330 35423 X

1 3 5 7 9 8 6 4 2

A CIP catalogue record for this book is available from
the British Library.

Typeset by CentraCet Limited, Cambridge
Printed and bound in Great Britain by
Mackays of Chatham plc, Chatham, Kent

For Bill and Tally

Thanks to Juliette B., Emily C., David H., John M. and Leonard S. for allowing me to visit their studios, and to Allison D. for her editorial contributions.

Confessions of an Accidental Terrorist

Mary Alice Baker

For Florence Alice Baker

I don't have any experience writing stuff down. I like to take photographs. That's how I see things. Don't know how to go about telling my life story. Most days I spend staring at photographs taped to the walls, thinking about the way things turned out. Some of the photographs are self-portraits I took my last month on the outside, when everything started to change. The way I looked, how I thought, everything. There's a picture of my friend Cass, then one of my mom, took it the last time I had dinner home. A couple newspaper and magazine clippings are up there too. They remind me how infamous I've become, how a nice girl like me wound up in a place like this.

The first picture on the wall, I look like I'm about seventeen years old going to a Hallowe'en party. I took it one day at Hansel & Gretel's Baby Photo Studio, where I used to work. The owner, who was kind of deranged, called Hansel & Gretel's the first theme-park baby photo studio, had little rooms built to look like the fairy tale and equipped each with a camera and minimum wage kid dressed up like Hansel or Gretel. I was one of the Gretels. His idea was make the kids want to smile, do volume business at the same time. He used to say to us, *You smile the kid smiles, the kid smiles the parent smiles, you're not just taking baby photos, you're in the smiling business.*

In the photograph, my blonde hair is in pigtails, I have red rouge shaped like big dots on my cheeks, wear a green jumper, a little yellow Gretel hat. My arms are akimbo and I'm smiling. I look like one of those wooden dolls on strings, only you can't see who's holding the strings, making me dance. I worked there three years, got as high as assistant manager, made nine dollars seventy-five cents an hour, minus tax. More money than I ever thought I'd make.

The last day I worked there, July it was, a customer came into the studio with his little boy. The boy was about three years old, had dark brown eyes, a wild spray of hair at the crown of his head. The customer gripped the boy by his wrist, carried him into the shop that way. The boy's shoes flailed two inches above the ground like he was hung on a rope. The customer slung the boy onto the desk, told him to shut up. The kid hadn't said a word. I listened to the customer tell me what he wanted, smiled, pretended I hadn't heard it all a million times before. The kind of guy thinks smacking his kid around teaches him to be a man, that was him.

The boy fidgeted like all kids do, thought better, stopped, stared ahead. I caught his eye, gave him the bright flash of teeth we called the portrait smile, because it usually makes the kid smile back and you can take the picture with him looking happy. This convinces grandma and grandpa and all the aunts and uncles that the kid is the darlingest angel on earth, even if he is in the middle of developing neuroses going to torment him the rest of his life. The boy lit up seeing me smile. I lifted my hand to give him a reassuring pat. Normal enough thing to do to a kid. But the boy jerked away. It wasn't just shyness. I saw the change come over his eyes. He was afraid. Thought I was going to hit him. I'd seen it before. A kid gets slapped around all the time, any sudden movement at his face and he flinches.

I led the boy down the gingerbread path, didn't stop at the Black Forest, the Gingerbread House, the Witch's Kitchen, we went straight into the studio outfitted like Hansel's Toyshop. I hoped the toys might bring him out. Hansel's Toyshop had three standard shots. Kid on rocking horse, kid on tricycle, kid with giant stuffed tiger. The boy gave the rocking horse a push, watched the carved wooden head bob up and down. His father coaxed him, slapped the saddle a couple times. The boy's eyes wandered, saw the giant tiger, looked up at me. I gave him an encouraging nod. He went after the tiger in that quick scrambling way little kids can move. His dad stood up, walked over, jerked the boy by his arm, sat him down on the rocking horse. The boy let out a shriek went through me like a bullet.

The picture of my mom, she was standing at the sink, doing dishes. I had a roll of high-speed black and white film in my camera. The look is big-grained, jagged, dark. Mom was turning toward me when I took the exposure. The movement blurs the vertical black and white stripes of her apron. She holds a stainless steel saucepan in a dishrag under her right arm, cradles it with all the tenderness of a mother and child. The kitchen light shines above and to the left of her head. The light glances white hot across the side of her face, drops into deep shadow where the slope of her forehead crests. The eye nearest the light is trapped by the washed-out brightness of her skin. The other eye is completely lost to darkness.

I took the picture before a dinner of pork chops, applesauce, mashed potatoes and buttered green beans. Pop was there. So was my oldest brother, Ray. Pop and Ray are machinists together in the same factory. Pop walked into the kitchen about six p.m., still in his work clothes, snapped a bottle of Bud out of the fridge, sat at the kitchen table. Mom and I were peeling potatoes, talking just to talk. We shut up when he came through the door.

He turned the kitchen chair around so he could prop up his elbow while he drank, coiled an arm around the rungs on the back of the chair for balance. The muscles of his arms flexed below rolled-up sleeves, made the tattoo wolf on his biceps strut. In between slugs, he tapped the base of the beer bottle against the back of the chair, the rhythm slow, like the drumbeat of a slave galley.

I'm his youngest child. I'm not sure he really ever liked me much, but I could get away with things the others couldn't. My sister, she wound up being not much good, up in Washington state somewhere drinking her life away. My other two brothers have problems too, don't come around anymore. I was the normal one. I was the one without problems. I was the one who tried to sweet-talk Pop out of his angrys. That was my role. I walked up behind, kissed him on the cheek. He wiped at the spot like I left some lipstick behind, wanted to rub it out. I messed his hair a little. He pushed me away, gave me a hard stare, said, "The way you come begging around the house, worse than a cat rubbing for table scraps."

"I was invited."

"Who invited you?"

"You did."

"I musta been drunk."

He was. A couple minutes after he said I should come again for dinner, he passed out on the kitchen table. He called that falling asleep after work. But I didn't say anything about it. I was a good girl. Talked like one. Looked like one. Long blonde hair, pink lipstick, matching nails, just a trace of eye-liner, matching heart earrings, pink cotton blouse, knee-length skirt, espadrilles.

Pop said, "Maybe if you knew how to cook for yourself, you'd find a man, not come pestering us all the time."

I answered, "Not my fault there's no men out there like you."

Pop put the beer bottle to his lips, said, "Goddamn right."

WHAM! A sudden impact noise turned our heads. It was Mom. She was tenderizing the meat. The pork chops were spread out on wax paper. She had a wooden mallet in her hand, was laying into the pork chops like driving railroad spikes. I wondered what she thought about every time she raised the mallet and brought it down.

Pop nudged Ray, who sat the next chair over, quiet as a mirror image. He said, "The girls nowadays, they all gotta be career girls."

Ray was thirty-eight and a bachelor, which Pop didn't think was right. To Pop's way of thinking, Ray should be married, and would be, if the present generation of women was any damn good. But Ray was a strong worker and his own man, so Pop never pressed him much. Ray hardly ever answered Pop directly. A grunt or shrug was about as vocal as he got. It avoided argument. I think that was the secret to his sticking around so long.

Pop said, "The girls nowadays, they got no time for men, unless it's time to screw. Isn't that right?"

He stared straight at me when he said this, dared me to talk back. I just wanted to stay out of trouble. I chopped the green beans for Mom, slivered some almonds to mix with the beans later. Pop got another beer from the fridge, sat back down. I felt his eyes on my back as I lit the gas and dropped the butter into the pan, to mix with the green beans. Mom and I glanced at each other, wondered if it was safe to talk. Talk was important to us. The subject didn't matter as much as the talking. It was the first Thursday in the month, when she always went to the hairdresser, so I said her hair looked great. Mom gave the bouffant a reassuring pat, asked, "You have a good day at work today?"

I didn't tell her about the boy, what happened in the studio. I didn't tell her I didn't like working there anymore but didn't know what else to do. It's never any fun listening to somebody complain about what a rotten job they have. When I talked about work, I tried to make it sound exciting, because I think Mom was proud that I was a professional photographer, no matter how low on pay and prestige.

"You two keep gabbing, we're never gonna get to eat," Pop said.

WHAM! Mom went back to pounding the pork chops.

Pop half-shouted across the kitchen, "Hey! You still going out with that bum, what's-his-name?"

"Which particular bum you talking about?"

"You know which one. The kid with the motorcycle. The one looks like he was born out of a pig's asshole."

Pop meant Wrex. Wrex was sort of my boyfriend. I say sort of because we'd only been going together for two months, and Wrex wasn't too dependable. He probably had other girls besides me, even if I never caught him with one. Pop knew about him because he saw us together once on Wrex's bike. Pop couldn't really do anything because I was twenty-four, had my own apartment. But if he'd ever caught me with a guy like Wrex when I was seventeen, I'd've got the crap beat out of me.

I said, "Me and Wrex are just friends."

I lied a lot around my family, to make things go easier.

Pop said, "I should hope to hell so. I should hope to hell you still got a little common sense left."

Ray grunted. That was his way of agreeing. Ray looks just like Pop. Dresses like him. Wears his hair like him. Except he doesn't talk as much, doesn't get the same case of angrys Pop gets. The big difference in our ages meant he wasn't around much when I was growing up. He joined the navy when I was just a baby. Did four tours of duty, then quit to join my Pop at the machine shop, turning out custom parts as a subcontractor for Northrop during the boom-boom years of defense spending, when the government was throwing dollars at everything that promised to gun down, run over, spy on and blow up the Soviets.

There was something about the way Pop and Ray were sitting that I wanted to hold in my hand and study. I went to get my camera bag. I knew Pop would get angry if I brought out my camera, because he didn't like me taking pictures. He couldn't understand it was an obsession for me. He thought a camera was something you took out when somebody had a birthday or came to visit. The idea I took photos to understand things about the world and myself made him suspicious, like maybe I was too stupid to understand that the world is a straightforward place where you have to work hard and support yourself and your family and then relax a little after, and art is for people who don't have to work for a living and unnecessary to guys like him, unless you consider television or action pictures art. Once, when I was about sixteen, I tried showing him some photos I took. He looked at them for half a minute, said I shouldn't waste my time. It used to hurt me. Now I've accepted it's just the way he is, and when I started to work at Hansel & Gretel's, photography suddenly became more okay with him, because I was making some money at it. He could understand working for money, where he couldn't understand working to be something you weren't, but wanted to be.

I composed the picture in my head before I took the camera from my bag. I wanted to take the shot looking up at Pop's pit-bull profile. I wanted him to look power-ful, legs sprawled, right elbow resting on the chair-back, hand cupped around a beer as he watched Mom off camera. Ray I placed in the right background, his clothes, hairstyle and posture an exact echo of Pop's, down to the way they held their beer bottles with the label facing the palm. I set the f-stop and shutter speed inside my bag, like I was rummaging for something. Then I lifted the camera, framed, pulled the trigger.

It was the shot I wanted, but then something more interesting happened. Pop's head snapped around. His eyes raged cinder-black, like I just slapped him. I took the second shot when the motion of Ray's head toward the camera changed his face to a confused blur. I pulled the trigger a third time. In the photograph, Pop's face streaks angrily away, and Ray stares at the camera, his pain and fear sharply etched upon the film. After I developed the roll, I couldn't decide which shot I liked best, so printed them together, as a triptych. It expresses a lot about how I feel toward my father.

The dinner didn't go very well after I took out the camera. Pop didn't say much, Ray didn't talk at all. When Mom or I said anything, Pop glared. It shut us up. I couldn't eat, watched him polish off two, three pork chops.

Pop said, "What're you looking at?"

I said, "Nothing."

Pop said, "You think I'm some kind of animal in a zoo?"

I said, "No, sir."

Pop said, "Then stop looking at me and eat."

I said, "Yes, sir."

I lifted my fork, speared a single green bean, chewed it around.

Pop said, "I don't want you taking pictures in the house anymore."

I didn't say anything, hoped if I didn't move, didn't breathe, he'd go away.

"Did you hear what I said, Mary?"

His saying my name was a sign of trouble. It was the kind of situation I used to clown my way out of, put on a little girl's voice to make him smile, say, "You jus' a gwumpy owld baar, Popykins, gwowlin' an' bein' scary, but you can't foo' me." I didn't say it this time, and he knew I wasn't saying it.

He said, "You got something to say to me, say it."

I didn't say it. I didn't look in his eye, because when Pop was angry you never looked in his eye.

"You got nothing to say? Then pass the pork chops."

I said, "Get the pork chops yourself."

He dropped his fork on the plate. It sounded like a gunshot.

"You do what I goddamn tell you to do or you'll get out of the goddamn house."

I backed my chair away, stood and said, "You want me out? Fine."

Pop reached across the table, grabbed my arm, squeezed hard, stared hard. Mom looked down at her plate. Ray sat still as a snapshot, a rough wedge of pork chop suspended between his plate and mouth. My arm burned, I could feel the muscles crush and bleed, the bones snap.

Pop said, "Sit. Down."

I wished I had a camera in my hands to pull the trigger on him, so I could look at the images after, try to figure out where his anger came from. It didn't make any sense, his anger. It didn't come from us, his family. We were all terrified of him. It came from someplace else, deep inside like a beast roaring and clawing to get out of his chest.

I sat down.

He said, "Now. Apologize."

I said, "I . . . I . . . I . . . I," like I was some kinda stuck record.

Mom said, "Please, dear, she's crying."

"I don't give a good goddamn what she's doing, she's gonna apologize or she's gonna sit here all night."

I said, "I'm sorry."

"Apology accepted. Now pass me the pork chops."

I passed him the pork chops, stared at my plate, listened to the sound of meat cut, chewed, swallowed. I asked, "Can I please be excused?"

Pop said, "No. Eat."

Mom said, "Please, you see she's upset."

"You taking her side now?"

Nobody said anything. Pop slammed his palm flat on the table. The dishes, glasses jumped. I jumped.

Pop said, "Okay, go on. You're excused."

I ran out of the house.

Like I said before, I have the photograph of Mom up on the wall here. The photograph is about many things to me, but now it talks mostly about disappearing. Because the person in my Mom seems to be erased by the light on the left side of her face, and swallowed by shadow on the right. The film has trapped her in the act of vanishing. I notice now that the vertical black and white stripes on her apron are like the bars that surround me. I've stared at the photograph for over a year now, and I still find something new.

2

Wrex's big black and chrome Harley was parked by the curb when I got to my apartment. One thing I could count on with Wrex, he never strayed far from his bike. I parked my Honda Civic hatchback at the rear of the building, circled around to the front. Wrex met me by the steps, wrapped his big arms around my waist and he kissed me a good kiss, said, "I need you to do something for me."

That kind of talk always meant trouble around Wrex. I pushed away, hiked up the stairs to my apartment. When I got the keys out of my purse, Wrex leaned back on the door, blocked the doorknob with his hips.

He said, "I need you to take a package to the airport tomorrow."

I tried to shove him away from the door, but he swiveled his hips so I couldn't key the lock, said not until I kissed him. I gave in and kissed him, grabbed his belt and pulled him away from the doorknob, pushed the door open and ducked inside my apartment.

Wrex stood in the open doorway, watched me as I dropped my purse and kicked off my pumps. He said, "As a gentleman, I can't enter a lady's apartment unless invited."

I laughed, because Wrex looked more like a barbarian raider come to kill the men, rape the women, and steal the children than any gentleman I'd ever seen. Black Doc Martens laced halfway up his calves. His blue jeans were torn at the knee, again just below the butt. A silver eagle belt-buckle jutted above his 501 button fly. His black leather jacket, worn all seasons regardless of temperature, was parted to a ripped white t-shirt. He hadn't shaved in three days, in fact he always hadn't shaved in three days, I wondered how he managed to keep his stubble at the same precise length every time I saw him. He liked fashion scars. Two big silver rings in his left ear, one in his right. A cobra on his right biceps, a jaguar on his left, the lightning-bolt logo of AC/DC on his butt, a name he discovered too late also meant lack of sexual preference. A red handkerchief swirled pirate-like around his head so often I began to suspect he was bald underneath. Later, after I had seen a dozen young men dressed like this in Hollywood, I realised Wrex wasn't dangerous in the way I thought. He just knew how to accessorize danger. But for my home town, Wrex was very extreme. And so I thought, very sexy.

The way he stood in the doorway, leaning on his elbow against the doorjamb, his hand cocked on his hip, gave me strong ideas how I wanted to spend the next hour. I grabbed his belt-buckle and pulled him inside, shut the door behind us. Wrex lowered his eyelids, so his eyes looked like two ripe bruises. I could have gone for him right there on the floor. I waited for him to kiss me. But he didn't kiss me.

He asked, "So can you do it?"

"Do what?"

"Take a package to the airport tomorrow."

"Got better things to do with my day off, thanks."

"But, babe, this is important."

"You don't think my day off is important?"

He looked all hurt, like I thought only about myself, didn't care about him. Typical. If he didn't sulk, he cried *but babe* this, and *but babe* that. He said, "Of course it is. If this wasn't even more important, I wouldn't ask you." This was a lie, because Wrex was so lazy he would flick his cigarette ashes on the floor where he sat rather than get up to find an ashtray, and if I complained about it, he'd flick them onto the leg of his jeans.

I said, "You got a bike. You take it."

"Just can't. Got things to do, you know. Important things."

I walked into the kitchen, which in my apartment

isn't much of a walk, more like an obstacle course depending on how much junk I've scattered on the floor, and poured myself a Jack Daniels on the rocks. Wrex had big ears, appeared at the kitchen door, asked, "You pouring two?"

"Maybe."

Wrex moved toward me with that sexy smile of his, something between a leer and outright amusement. He wrapped his arms around me from behind, nibbled at the back of my neck while I tried to sip at my drink. I forgot about the drink and we kissed. After a while Wrex pulled back, asked, "So you can do it?"

Like me kissing him meant something different than him kissing me, like it meant yes I kissed him so I'd do what he wanted. I said, "No time. I'm going to the mall, taking photographs."

Wrex pulled his arms away and stomped out of the kitchen. It looked like I was getting a fight whether I wanted one or not. If I was, I wasn't going to chase it around the apartment. I leaned against the counter, drank bourbon. Wrex's boots clomped first one way, then the other across the living room. He didn't hold out for long. I didn't expect him to, not with the bourbon still in the kitchen.

"Alright, fuck it, I'll pay your gas money." This said in a pissed-off voice, like it was a major concession I was asking and he wasn't going to take one step more.

"I said I was shooting pictures."

I handed him a drink and sat on the living-room floor.

He said, "So shoot 'em out at the airport."

"Doesn't work that way."

"Damn but you're a stubborn bitch!"

"You wanna sleep on your bike tonight, just keep talking."

This was a very effective threat with Wrex because his landlord booted him out of his apartment for chronic non-payment and he didn't have a place to crash except with me or a friend named Dan, who wasn't always so happy to see him. Wrex never had any money, though he always claimed he was going to score the next day because there was this guy owed him big time and was going to pay him back. But whenever I went out with him to collect the guy never showed up. Sometimes I think Wrex invented the whole situation so I wouldn't think he was a total loser.

He sat cross-legged on the floor in front of me, said, "You know I just talk like that and don't mean it."

I couldn't stay mad at him for long, not when he looked at me with his big brown eyes all sad. He had that combination of rebel good looks, don't-give-a-shit attitude, and little-boy sensitivity that's always sucked the heart out of me. I got up to pour us another drink. Wrex put an old Led Zeppelin tape on, something we both liked. We drank instead of argued for a while. I relaxed.

Wrex didn't. The second song into the tape he slammed his hand down on the carpet, said, "I really need you to do this for me."

"I'm busy, and gas money isn't going to make me unbusy."

"Okay. How 'bout ten dollars?"

I gave him the scornful look such a low figure deserved.

He sounded hopeful, asked, "Twenty?"

I thought I'd get him to scream, said, I'd do it for two hundred.

But Wrex didn't scream. He looked real worried for a couple seconds, a sudden creasing of his brow indicating serious dialog was taking place between his ears. He asked, "You mean, like, dollars?"

I nodded, amazed he was even thinking about it.

Wrex said, "Okay. We got a deal."

That got me to worrying. If Wrex was willing to pay that much, he was delivering something for somebody and was too smart or too scared to take it himself. I knew Wrex sold marijuana every now and then, not enough to be a real drug dealer, but if he found a good buy, he was known to pass it along to friends at a small profit. Not that I think that was necessarily a bad thing. Most of the people I went to school with smoked dope at least some of the time. I didn't smoke it myself. Not because of moral reasons, like I didn't do drugs because I thought they were evil. It wasn't because I was too good either, because even some good girls smoked every now and then. I was just afraid of them. I tried it once and I went a little crazy. But I didn't hold it against Wrex that he liked to do drugs as long as he wasn't stoned all the time, and if he sold a little every now and then on an approximate break-even basis it was okay by me. Maybe I even thought it was exciting, like maybe I went for Wrex because he did things I couldn't. But I didn't want to get involved in it, and I certainly didn't want to deliver a package of something that turned out to be drugs and then get arrested. That would be an irony I wouldn't appreciate. I said, "You gotta tell me, Wrex. What's in the package?"

"I can't tell you what's in the package," Wrex said.

"If you don't tell me, I don't go."

"Information, papers, that's what's in the package."

"What kind of information?"

"White collar stuff. Completely legit."

Wrex's eyes got that glazed-over look tells me to watch out. I told him two hundred bucks was more money than he'd made all year. He was either crazy or lying and probably both.

"I'm gonna tell you something, but you gotta promise not to repeat it to anybody, ever. Not that anything's illegal about what I'm gonna say, just that it's secret, and I could get into trouble for telling you."

I said, "Sure, I promise."

"I'm being followed."

"Uh-huh."

"No, really. I've been doing some jobs for this company. It's spooky stuff. Some companies got spy networks just like the CIA. And if they're afraid of getting caught, they use somebody like me, somebody from outside the company, somebody untraceable. Because I mean, hey, they all got big cars and houses and the last thing they wanna do is get sued."

"Go to jail, you mean."

"No really, it's not that kind of illegal."

"Then what kind of illegal is it?"

"No kind at all. This company I'm freelancing with, it's got a secret deal with somebody coming to the airport tomorrow. But with me being followed no way I can meet him."

"So lose them on your bike."

"Can't. If I make any sudden moves, they'll be sure to know something's up. I gotta stay here, be the decoy. And I'd still have to rent a car, because the package I gotta pick up is too big to fit on my bike. It needs a car."

"Pick up? What package?" I asked, confused, because at first I thought there was only one package, and now there seemed to be two.

"The other guy is bringing something and I'm supposed to trade what I've got for what he's got."

"Then what's in his package?"

"Don't know. Something from overseas. We meet at the International Terminal."

I said, "Drugs come from overseas."

"Look, if the US Government lets it pass through customs, that should make it legal enough. You want them maybe to put a stamp on, says, *Legal enough for Mary Baker?*"

I went to get the bottle, poured us both three fingers of bourbon. What Wrex was telling me had to be partly true, because Wrex wasn't capable of inventing a story that sounded so wild. Wrex's imagination generally limited his lies to the yes or no category, with an occasional embellishment easy to spot for its lack of sense. The more I drank the safer the whole idea sounded. Not that I use the alcohol as an excuse for lack of good judgment. I didn't completely believe Wrex about the whole thing being absolutely legal, but I didn't see how I could get into any trouble unless things weren't what Wrex said, so I said yes, I'd deliver the package. Then we drank and argued about how he was going to pay me. I wanted it all up front, because Wrex had this tendency to be broke all the time and not pay the money he owed. Wrex swore he didn't have a dime on him but he'd pay after delivery, really, but I stuck to my guns, two hundred now or no deal, until finally he pulled out his wallet, threw two portraits of Benjamin Franklin onto the floor. Then Wrex picked me up, carried me off to bed like I was his whore and he'd just paid me. And that was pretty much how he acted in bed. He treated me like a convenience store he was in and out so fast. Then he fell asleep.

I was going to say what the hell, I want a little more attention, or at least love and affection after, maybe you shouldn't fall on me and just lie there when you're finished. But I didn't say anything. I stayed awake half the night, crushed under the weight of his arm thrown across my chest, suffocated by the heavy sound of his breathing, thinking, this had to be love, or else why did I put up with it?

3

I woke the next morning to speed metal playing full blast on the stereo. Wrex shouted a cheery good morning, threw half my wardrobe out the closet, told me I had to get dressed so I'd be ready to leave for the airport by ten-thirty. I glanced at the clock. Seven-thirty. Only gave me three hours to get ready. I called him some names, told him if he didn't get lost, make me some coffee, I was going back to sleep, he could take his stupid package to the airport himself. That was the last I heard of him for ten minutes or so, when I heard knocking at the bath-room door. I opened it to a steaming cup of coffee in Wrex's hands.

"I know you know everything already, but I thought you might want to hear that I hafta go get the package now, and the reason I woke you early was because I wanted to make sure you'd be up and ready to go when I came back."

I sipped at the coffee. It wasn't half-bad. I leaned through the crack in the door to kiss him thanks. He was so stiff I checked my lips for splinters. I asked, "What are you so nervous about?"

Wrex ran to the bedroom door, said, "I'm not nervous. Everything has to go right is all, I'll be back by nine-thirty at the latest." Then he was gone and things were quiet.

I took the coffee into the bedroom, thought about what I should wear. It was an adventure I was dressing for, I wanted to look mysterious. But I didn't own anything mysterious. Just stuff made me look like a small-town girl takes pictures of babies for a living. I settled on a white skirt and black blouse, a scratched pair of checker-board sunglasses I found on the street once and threw into a drawer, a floppy straw hat I wore a couple times a year when I didn't want any sun. If I couldn't look mysterious at least I'd look disguised.

I looked at the clock, saw I had an hour to kill before Wrex got back, wanted to tell Mom I was sorry about last night. They lived a five-minute drive away, just around the block by California standards. Easy enough to drive there, say hi, get back before Wrex knew I was gone. I wrote a quick note saying I'd be back in five minutes, left it pinned to the door in case Wrex got back early.

Mom's ten-year-old Buick Skylark was parked in the drive when I pulled up to the house. Pop's half-ton was gone. He left for work every weekday morning at half-past seven, Mom at nine. I leaned on the doorbell a few times, daydreamed about going to the beach after I dropped Wrex's package. I'd take my camera along, get some crowd shots, maybe the sunset would be good. Nobody answered the door. Mom never went anywhere far without her car. Probably at the neighbors', having a quick chat before work. I had a key to the front door, so I went in, thought I'd wait ten minutes to see if she showed up, leave a note on the kitchen table saying I dropped by if she didn't.

The kitchen table had been cleared and wiped, but half the dishes were stacked unwashed to the side of the sink. Mom never left the kitchen until it was spotless. It was probably my fault. I got Pop so riled up she retreated to her bedroom for some peace and quiet. I soaped up a sponge and washed dishes, read for the thousandth time Mom's framed needlepoint Serenity Prayer pinned to the cabinet at eye level: *God grant me the courage to change the things I can, the patience to accept the things I can't, and the wisdom to know the difference.* Mom always liked to buy knick-knacks with inspiring or religious messages. She scattered them all over the house, but mostly in the bathroom and kitchen. The memento to the right of the sink was a big ceramic tile. A woodsy home was painted on it, smoke pouring from the chimney, a picket fence wrapping a green front lawn. Above the roof, the words GOD BLESS THIS HAPPY HOME arched like a rainbow. Mom had cut an old picture of me and Pop so just our bodies were left, glued us to the corner of the tile, inside the picket fence. The photograph was taken by the lake one winter, when I was about seven years old. I wear a ski-cap that's a couple sizes too big. Pop has his arm around me. We're both smiling as wide as our mouths will go. We look like a good father and daughter. We look happy.

When I finished the dishes I sat down to write the note. Before I figured out what to write, I got up and walked around the house. It wasn't that I heard anything. I walked through the living room to the master bedroom. The door was closed. I knocked softly. Nobody answered. I opened the door anyway. Mom's hair poked out of the covers. She was lying on her side, facing the wall.

"Mom?" I called, soft in case she was still sleeping.

"Afraid I've got a virus, honey. You shouldn't get too close, 'cause it might be catching."

"Nonsense. You tell me what you need, I'll get it for you."

I hurried around to her side of the bed. She hid her face under the covers, but not fast enough for me to miss why she was sick.

Mom said, "I don't need anything, thanks."

The tip of her elbow stuck out to where I could see it. She was wearing her work blouse. She'd been up, tried to hide when she heard me coming through the front door. When she realized I already knew, she let go her hold on the covers. She lay huddled up in a little ball, ashamed. I'd seen him do worse, but this was bad enough. The pouch of skin below her left eye had swollen to a purple bruise. The bruise stretched to her temple and brow, slit her eye like a crescent moon.

Mom said, "He didn't mean to do it."

I curled up beside her on the bed, wrapped my arms around her shoulders from behind. Looking at her eye made me feel a little sick. It was my fault she got hit. If I hadn't come over for dinner, if I hadn't smarted back, if I hadn't run out of the house. I knew what could happen. My fault.

Mom said, "I shoulda known better. You can't talk to that man when he gets mad. I shoulda gone into the spare bedroom and waited for him to simmer down."

I didn't have to ask what happened. Pop cooled to a slow burn. Ray left. Mom said something good about me, thought she could get him to forgive. Pop said he never wanted to see me again. That was what he said when somebody in the family talked back. That was what he said to Sharon, my other brothers George and Charley. Mom protested it wasn't fair. Pop said I'll show you fair and smacked her. Maybe he was sorry after. But just once was all it took. He hit hard.

I held onto her for a long while.

Mom kissed my arm, said, "You've always been a good girl."

My fault.

The phone rang. When I sat up, I saw the clock. Ten. I caught Mom's hand as she reached for the phone, gave her a hug, scrambled out the door.

Mom said, "Well, for heaven's sake." That was what she almost always says when something surprises her, when she can't quite believe how crazy something is. Sometimes, late at night when I'm alone and can't sleep, I curl myself around the little things she used to say, expressions without meaning mostly, except the goodness of her heart. It makes me feel less alone.

When I got back to the apartment Wrex's complexion had turned the color of the ash on the end of his cigarette, four butts lay crushed out on my doorstep. He clutched a briefcase tightly to his chest. The first thing he wanted to know was where I'd been, but it was clear from his tone of voice he didn't really want an answer. He just wanted to criticize me for leaving when I wasn't supposed to.

I opened the door, said, "None of your business where I've been."

"None of my business! You go skipping off with my two hundred dollars, half-kill me with worry, and it's none of my business?"

I gave him a look. A short one. One that said I was in no mood. He set the briefcase on the kitchen table. I reached for it, thought maybe I'd try the lock, see what was inside, but he slapped my hand away. He said for me not to touch anything, just pay attention. I asked why he hit me.

"Don't do this to me, not now," Wrex said.

"You hit me and I can't even ask why?"

"I didn't hit you."

"You sure did."

"I'm not going to waste time arguing about it."

"You hit me and now you won't even talk about it?"

"Hey, I'm sorry, I love you with all my heart and soul, but please, babe, have a little mercy here. I'm just trying to get the job done. For a couple minutes don't say anything, just listen for once, okay? You can yell at me later, but now, we gotta get moving."

I said, "Go ahead. I'm listening."

Wrex said the briefcase was locked. He didn't know the combination, I was under no circumstances to try to open it. I was to take the briefcase to the departure-level lobby of the International Terminal, which is on the top tier of the airport, and look for a man in his early forties. The man would be wearing a blue business suit and yellow tie and holding an unlit cigar. I was to go up to the guy and tell him he was in a no-smoking area. The guy would say the cigar isn't lit. Then I'd hand him the briefcase, and he'd give me a package in return.

Wrex reached into his jacket for a plain white envelope, handed it to me. I held it up to the light, couldn't see anything through the paper, asked, "What's in it?"

"I don't know, I don't wanna know, and you don't wanna know either. Don't get smart and try to open it. Give it to the guy at the airport."

Wrex took the briefcase from the kitchen table and pushed me toward the door, because it was already a few minutes past ten-thirty, and I absolutely had to meet the guy at noon, not a minute later, or, Wrex said, the whole deal could blow up in smoke. I grabbed the floppy hat, sunglasses, my camera bag and portfolio. As I loaded the stuff into the car, Wrex made me repeat everything I was supposed to say and do at the airport. Maybe I didn't have the self-confidence to do well in school, but I'm not stupid and I'm sure as hell smarter than Wrex, so I started changing the story around just to see if he'd notice, giving the guy a blue tie and a yellow suit. Wrex thought I was seriously confused, his expression was so anxious I broke out laughing. He laughed along, sounding sick about it. When I started the engine, Wrex motioned for me to open the window. I did and he said to be careful. Then Wrex kissed me. Judas never kissed so good.

4

My town never amounted to much, just a small town over the hills from LA with a main street and a corner grocer and little shops owned by people who live there and a sign at the city limits says the town's motto, *Small Towns are Smile Towns*. About a dozen years ago we got surrounded by freeway commuters wanting to escape the city. The commuters made a little town for themselves has nothing to do with us. Doesn't have a main street. Has mini-malls and supermarkets and fast food franchises and a fancy shopping center with a cineplex and stores like Hansel & Gretel's. The freeway runs right next to it. Makes it easier for the commuters to get home in a hurry. Last stoplight before the freeway, I thought about opening the envelope, decided I shouldn't. I stuffed the envelope in the crevice between the briefcase and the seat-back, got on the freeway going south to Los Angeles International Airport.

Lot of girls I knew in high school wanted a commuter's son for a boyfriend, figured it was how to get to the other side of the freeway. I never knew any commuters except to say hello. Ever since I was little, I always figured I was going to get blue-collar married, move to a rickety tract home, work some kind of retail job days, raise a family nights. Most of the kids I went to school with married early, or left town a couple years back. I hung on, not going anywhere, not having any ideas of a real career until I got the job at Hansel & Gretel's. Taking pictures of babies wasn't all that bad as far as work went. I didn't know enough to be humiliated. I needed the job. Nobody ever told me I'd be any good at anything, so I was proud to be a good Gretel. It was a delicate balance, knowing the precise moment to snap the shutter before the little darlings began to drool or whine or wail with such eardrum-splitting ferocity the memory is enough to make me reach for the nearest birth-control device. I never dreamed of becoming a real photographer, but it seemed possible that I might succeed assisting other photographers, maybe have my own portrait studio some day. But I needed a lot of money for that, with few prospects of ever making more than just enough to get by.

I pulled the envelope out of the crevice, set it flat on the briefcase. I wasn't so stupid I didn't know what was in the envelope. I was giving a locked briefcase to somebody, and how was that somebody going to open it unless the answer was in the envelope? I held it up to the blue sky above the steering wheel, still couldn't see the writing inside. If I wanted to know what was in the briefcase, I had to figure some way to open the envelope.

I pulled off the freeway, popped the hood, twisted the radiator cap just a notch. Did it just to see if it could be done, if I could get away with it. A thin jet of steam hissed from the opening. Then I ran the flap of the envelope back and forth across the steam, until the gum holding it down started to dissolve. Slipped my fingernail into the seam. The flap lifted easily off the back of the envelope, except for one part where I had to tear it a little.

I went back inside the car, shook out a single sheet of paper. Three numbers were typed on the upper third: 9-1-3. Not a good omen. Numbers one and three together looked like thirteen, add up all three numbers, thirteen again. Gave me some serious thoughts maybe I wasn't doing the right thing, opening the case. But I didn't open it much, just a crack to see what was inside. Then I shut the case, started the Honda and pulled back onto the freeway. I thought about places I could go, places I could hide and still have a good time. Places like Paris, Mexico, South America. Because what I saw in the case was money. Stacks and stacks of what looked like hundred dollar bills. Problem was, I'd never been anywhere, didn't know anything about Paris or Mexico or South America except they didn't speak English and I sure as hell didn't speak French or Spanish. I had an old boyfriend moved to Bakersfield. Didn't think I'd want to hide out there. Could be a million bucks on the seat next to me, and I couldn't think of anyplace to go with it. Goes to prove I'm basically honest, couldn't imagine really stealing it, didn't want Wrex on my conscience because if I stole the money they'd probably break his legs or worse.

So I drove. It was already noon. I drove like hell. Didn't matter how fast I drove, I was half an hour late. I hit the top tier at LAX doing seventy, cut across three lanes of traffic and double-parked near the International Terminal. About six other cars were double-parked ahead of me. I grabbed the briefcase and envelope, stepped out of the car, and you know how sometimes your ear picks out certain sounds? That afternoon it was the airport recording, *The white zone is for the loading and unloading of passengers only*. The voice in the recording sounds harmless but means if you leave your car unattended, some cop is going to give it a parking ticket. That was on the back of my mind as I walked into the terminal and looked for the guy I was supposed to meet, just the thing I needed was to get a parking ticket after breaking every traffic law in the book getting there.

My contact looked to be a guy standing under the TV sets that tell you when the planes leave. I hung back for a moment to check him out. Blue suit, yellow tie. He was pretty big, about six feet tall, two hundred pounds, face gone beefy red like you see when older guys eat and drink too much, don't work out. He was waving his cigar back and forth like he was having a nicotine fit. I walked up to him, said what I was supposed to say about smoking in a no-smoking area. He just about shouted at me the fucking cigar wasn't fucking lit, so who cares he was in a fucking no-smoking area? Had a funny accent, like he wasn't from around here, just discovered the F-word and wanted to try it out everywhere.

I said, "That wasn't exactly what you were supposed to say. You were supposed to just say, 'The cigar isn't lit.'"

"You were supposed to be here at noon, and you were supposed to be a man."

His *w*'s were funny too, sounded like *v*'s. I said, "Yeah, well, Wrex couldn't make it."

The contact said something I didn't understand, some kind of foreign language, and it didn't sound very nice. But I didn't want to make a scene, just wanted to get the transaction over with. I asked him where was the item I was supposed to pick up? He pointed to this big black case on wheels, more like a chest, stood about four feet high, looked like it weighed a couple hundred pounds.

"How am I supposed to get that into my car?" I asked him.

He looked at me like he couldn't believe I asked the

question. He said, "You tell Fleischer I don't like dealing with amateurs."

I told him I didn't know any Fleischers, maybe if he explained who the guy was, I could deliver the message. He called me an idiot, reached down and took the briefcase out of my hands. More like ripped it. Fine. If that was the way he wanted it, the sooner I got out of there, the better. I pushed the chest toward the glass doors out front. He grabbed me by the arm before I got more than a couple steps. It was rude, the way he grabbed my arm. I didn't like him touching me, and I almost popped him one right there, just planted my foot and let it rip, like my Pop taught me years ago, always hit off the back foot and twist your hip into it.

"The envelope!" the guy said. "How am I supposed to open the fucking briefcase without the fucking envelope?"

It was in my hand the whole time. It wasn't like I was trying to hide it. I slapped the envelope into his palm, noticed the moment it left my fingers the back flap hadn't sealed up exactly right. In fact, hadn't sealed up at all. He noticed it right away, said, "Hey, wait a minute!"

I rolled the case toward the entrance fast as I could. The contact would suspect I didn't stop at the envelope, I opened the briefcase too, maybe took a little something out. Wrex or his bosses could be double-crossing him. If money was missing, it would look like I'd stolen it. The contact started to come after me, but I wasn't going anywhere fast pushing that case. He decided to open the briefcase first, see if I'd stolen anything supposed to be in there.

Someone shouted, "Watch out!" because I was too busy looking back to watch where I was going. I pulled up just short of a woman must have been at least eighty, leaned on her cane she was so crippled with arthritis. I remember thinking, great, now I'm running down little old ladies, this is the last thing I'll ever let Wrex talk me into.

I thought the guy tackled me or something, I got hit so fast and hard I was in the air before I knew what happened. The sidewalk twisted underneath, came fast toward my head, and there was this moment when I felt my brain explode out my skull. Next thing I remember, I was sitting on the cement walkway, covered in shards of glass. It was quiet as I've ever heard it, not a sound, except this high-pitched tone in my ears. Nothing moved. The old woman sat next to me, perfectly fine except her eyes were glazed and mouth hung open. A jam of people lay jumbled together on the sidewalk, arms over their heads, except for two or three, who stood like surviving trees after a blast. Out on the traffic loop, a half dozen cars and a bus had skidded into one other. A puff of smoke drifted out of the International Terminal, front windows smashed to jagged teeth.

A calm voice broke the stillness, said, *The white zone is for the loading and unloading of passengers only.*

A woman screamed. One of the men got to his feet and walked toward the International Terminal. It was weird the way he walked, crouched low, as though expecting to get shot at. Then he ran, and a couple other guys got the same idea, started running too. People got out of their cars, glanced around, wondered what the hell happened. I pushed myself off the sidewalk, looked for my hat. I don't know why I wanted to find my hat just then. Didn't like it much, wore it only a couple times a year. Shock, I guess. The hat was under the wheel of a Chevy Blazer parked at the curb. I picked it up. Smoke gusted out of the terminal, hung heavy black against the sky. It wasn't until then I realized nobody tackled me. It was a bomb that exploded. And chances were pretty good the bomb was in the briefcase I carried all morning.

Your basic life training doesn't prepare you for what to do in situations like this. I stood by the curb, watched people go in and out of the terminal. Most of the people stumbling out had blood on them. Some of the people running in came back out, carrying people too hurt to walk by themselves. I followed the people running in. The sense was shocked out of me. I wanted to see what happened, maybe find the guy I gave the briefcase to. It was hard to see inside. Shadows howled around the smoky dark, insubstantial and noisome as ghosts. Fire skittered here and there along the ceiling. I wasn't thinking too clearly, but somewhere my brain told my lungs to hold still.

I knew about where the contact had been kneeling. He was near the TV monitors, but I couldn't find any TV monitors. My eyes burned. I couldn't hold my breath any more. The contact wasn't anywhere around I could see, at least no recognizable parts of him. I turned around to go back, couldn't decide which way back was. I took a couple steps one direction, stopped, took a couple steps another direction, stopped again. The ground felt strange, all crumbly. I looked down to my feet. The floor was gone. Blown out. Ground zero.

The first thing I did when I got outside was try to breathe, I had a good lungful of smoke, the air got me to coughing it out. Blood dripped onto the sidewalk at my feet. I wiped at my nose, got a bloody hand. Sirens wailed a ways off in the distance. It suddenly didn't seem like such a good idea for me to stick around. I didn't trust anybody to believe I was innocent just then. The smartest thing was to get away fast and worry about the consequences later. The black case lay flat on its side a few feet from where the blast first threw me. I didn't have any experience in the fugitive from justice thing, just what everybody knows watching television and the movies, but I knew it was dumb to leave anything behind could link me to what happened. I walked over, tried to lift it. The thing weighed a ton.

The thought came to me I should leave it there, wipe my prints from the handle and get the hell gone, when two guys came over and helped me tilt the thing back up onto its wheels. Didn't really see them until I'd already started lifting. I was about to say thanks when one of them called me a stupid bitch and the other pushed me and said I should get the fuck out of the way. I didn't get it. Here it was twice in one day somebody was cussing at me. First the guy with the accent and now these guys, both mid-thirties, balding and pot-bellied in identical rayon windbreakers and stay-press slacks, had mustaches looked like rat tails glued above their lips. A couple of real Frick and Fracks. I wasn't going to let anybody ugly and mean shove me around like I didn't exist. I yelled out they should stop, but all that did was make them push the case faster. I shouted at two airport cops running up the sidewalk, but they didn't pay any attention. The terminal was burning good, a lot of people were shouting things. I got an idea, yelled, "Looters!" I don't know if it was in some riot training film they saw, because both turned to see what I was talking about, then yelled stuff like "Police!" and "Freeze!" But the guys didn't freeze, they took off in opposite directions, had to abandon the case to get away.

The sirens were getting so loud I couldn't think, fire trucks and ambulances and cop cars weaving through traffic from both directions. All adrenaline, I hoisted the case up over the bumper and into the hatchback. The only idea I had was to get away, think someplace else. I jumped behind the wheel, swerved around the gawkers and parked cars, bounced over a sidewalk curb, sped out of traffic jammed in front of the terminal. Something pink flapped under my windshield wiper. An envelope of some kind. I laughed. Couldn't stop laughing the next five miles. A parking ticket. A half-hour ago the worst thing I thought could happen was a parking ticket, and here I'd got one.

5

I drove south on surface streets, through Inglewood to Torrance and Long Beach. Swung east through cities with exotic names that had nothing to do with what I was seeing, like Bellflower, Gardenia, Lawndale. After an hour or so in the car, everything started to look the same, four-lane boulevards stretching without dip or bend to the horizon, strip malls, fast food franchises, gas stations. I didn't think about what happened, didn't think about what I was going to do, other than follow the road I was on to the next and the next after that. You can drive forever in Los Angeles, never travel the same street twice. Somewhere around Downey I tired of the blood on my face, turned into a gas station to wash up.

The bathroom smelled heavy with urine, looked like it had been cleaned once this decade. I ran the tap, looked around the streaks of grease cutting across the mirror. My stomach twitched at the first good sight I got of my face. Tried to look just at the skin to scrub the blood off, but it didn't work. Kept seeing the whole face and the scared eyes. It was the last place I wanted to be sick but my stomach gave me no choice. I fell to my knees in front of the toilet and one whiff shot the contents out my stomach like a cannonball.

After cleaning up I felt better. I sat behind the wheel and searched through my purse for a piece of gum or candy to take the bad taste out of my mouth. My purse was crammed with stuff I suddenly didn't understand why I kept, melted lipstick, compact case, eyeliner, perfume, wadded-up tissues, ticket stubs, a self-help psychology book I'd wanted to read but never did, old parking tickets, loose tampons, keys I couldn't remember what they fit, a broken rabbit's foot, a Don't Worry Be Happy button Mom gave me, not a single lousy stick of gum or piece of candy. I dumped it all out onto the seat. Half-stuck to the bottom of my purse was a lint-covered Certs only a couple years old. I popped it into my mouth, shoved everything except my wallet onto the floor.

I knew Wrex crashed sometimes with this guy I said before was named Dan out in this small town north of where I lived. It wasn't much of a town, more like an outpost for white trash and young kids without much money, living in beat-up old houses. Dan's place was a one bath, three bedroom shack with a big old oak tree in the middle of a dirt yard. I parked down the street so I could watch the house. Saw nothing move except the neighborhood dogs, decided to walk up, check it out. The back door was wide open. I called, "Hey, anybody home?" a couple times, stepped inside.

At first I thought it was just the usual bachelor experiment in animal behavior, but half into the living room I knew different. The place was trashed. The sofa slashed, turned upside down. Shelves pushed over onto the floor. The TV set toppled onto its side. Clothes, records, CDs, magazines scattered over the carpet. I knew the house hadn't been ripped off because the stereo was there. Smashed to hell, but there. It looked to me like Wrex burned somebody in a drug deal. Wrex told me drug dealers sometimes trash a place if they feel ripped off. The drug deal had to be connected to the briefcase blowing up at the airport, it was probably heroin or cocaine in the black case now packed into the back of my Honda. Drug dealers trashed the place because Wrex didn't deliver the merchandise. If they caught him, they'd do worse to his body than what they did to this place. They'd do the same to me, if I was caught.

I drove south again on the Interstate, wanted to go home, pull the blankets over my head, make the world go away. If the drug dealers hadn't caught Wrex yet, they wouldn't know who I was or where I lived. It was too early to worry about the police. The police couldn't already know I was the one carried the bomb. They'd figure it out soon enough, because no way they were going to let anybody get away with something like bombing the airport. The FBI would come in, find a scrap of leather from the briefcase had my fingerprint on it. I had a couple days at least, no reason I couldn't go into my apartment, collect a few things, maybe even sleep for the night.

I parked down the street from my apartment building, watched the neighborhood, looked for anything different, any cars didn't look like they belonged, any people I didn't recognise. Nothing seemed out of the ordinary. Just the usual summer evening in a small town, stereo blasting somewhere down the street, kids cruising by in jacked-up Fords and chopped Chevys, a few guys drinking beers in the front yard. Everything seemed safe and familiar.

I climbed the stairs to my apartment, dreamed about a hot bath, a tall glass of Jack Daniels on ice. All I had with me was my keys. I looked carefully at my apartment window. The curtains were shut, just like I'd left them. I put my key to the lock, was about to turn the latch, when I noticed scratch marks on the door near the dead-bolt, a wedge-shaped indentation in the door frame. I didn't remember the marks being there before, and as I continued to rattle the lock, the marks looked more and more shaped like the head of a crow-bar somebody might use to pry open the door.

I've got a sixth sense tells me when a guy is watching, and it said an eye in the peephole watched every move I made. Some bastard was in my apartment, waiting for me to open the door. I backed away, spun toward the stairs, tried to keep fear from popping my thoughts out my head. One of the guys from the airport was coming up the front walk, Frick it was, which meant it was Frack behind the door watching me. Frick raised his hands like he meant me no harm, smiled, hoped this would make me trust him. But there was a menace behind the smile that I'd seen before in men who wanted to hurt me, and there was something about his pasty skin, lank hair, and skinny mustache that made me think he was a spadeful of earth away from the living dead.

He said, "Hey, little girl, you get curious, open that briefcase once when you were all alone?"

I shook my head, listened to the door opening behind me.

"Wasn't supposed to go off, you see, the first time. Was supposed to go off the second time, which means it was you or your boyfriend opened it." His eyes drifted over my shoulder to where I could hear Frack slipping out the door. He took two steps up, said, "Just stay right there, little girl, and I won't hurt you."

No way they were going to take me without a fight. I turned, swung hard on my heels, keys fisted like a brass knuckle. Frack ducked, afraid of getting raked, slipped on the welcome mat. Frick charged up the stairs to get me, yelling I was only a girl, for Chrissakes. I jumped the railing, fell forward after I hit ground, scraped elbows, knees, hands. The impact rattled every bone in my body and I knew it should hurt, but it didn't. Truth is I was so pumped full of adrenaline I didn't feel anything but fear. I rolled upright and ran to my Honda. Frick and Frack were slow coming off the stairs. I cranked the starter and the engine caught with a loud pop sounded like backfire. Hondas never backfire. There was another pop, a planking sound back in the hatch. I turned toward the sound. Frack stood in the middle of the street. The bastard had a gun, he was shooting at me. I stomped on the accelerator, wove all over the street as I took off. I didn't know whether to duck or just drive. I hunched over the steering wheel, shoulders rounded like you do when you expect to get hit from behind. When I didn't hear another shot, I glanced in the rearview mirror, saw Frick hopping into a complete citizen car, a brown Chevy Caprice, something you'd never pick out as suspicious on any street in the world.

My Honda didn't have the horses to outrun the Chevy if it got on my tail. I whipped left onto the first cross street, left again to double back. A Winnebago camper, big as a house, loomed up ahead, mid-block. I snuck around behind it, fast as a rabbit going to ground. Nothing I could do after that but wait it out, the idea they would see the first left turn but not guess the second, would figure I'd gone straight or turned right or done anything but double back. A couple minutes ticked off the clock, the most happily uneventful minutes of my life. I started moving again, stuck to back streets, snaked around the canyons to the Palmdale Freeway. I had a choice to drive east to Las Vegas maybe, or west the back way into Los Angeles.

I got off the Hollywood Freeway at Highland. Didn't know how to gamble, been to Hollywood a couple times with the gang on trips where we'd load up in somebody's car, pretend we weren't small town hicksters. I followed Highland down to Sunset Boulevard. My stomach growled. There was a strip-mall off to the right. I pulled into the lot, read the smorgasbord of choices advertised on the signboard, pizza and hamburgers and submarine sandwiches and Chinese take-out and frozen yogurt. Yogurt sounded about right, because my stomach was still pretty uptight, I wasn't sure how much I could eat.

The frozen yogurt shop was clean and bright. The girl behind the counter wore a pointed yellow hat and striped brown and yellow smock. The shop uniform. Looked like an overripe banana. She asked, "Hello, may I help you?" Her voice was cheerful, I could tell the manager made her practice. The manager would say, *Gotta make the customer feel special, happy he came in here, you're not just a yogurt scooper, you're in the happiness business.* I felt so sorry for her I almost walked out. But I needed to eat something, ordered a chocolate banana frozen yogurt, hid in the corner booth. I took a couple of bites, set the spoon aside, thought, okay, I'll turn myself in, tell the police it was all a big mistake, I'm really innocent, please don't throw me in jail. Yeah, right. I was pretty naive in those days, but not completely stupid. They gave the death penalty to assassins, terrorists, cop killers, drug murderers. I guessed I was two of the above. If the law could figure a way to execute somebody twice, I was going to be their girl. There was an outside chance I could cop a plea for testifying against Wrex, but Wrex looked like small fry in this whole deal. Wrex would be the one they'd get to cop a plea, he could nail Frick and Frack. And if the law didn't catch them, the only person they'd have to persecute for the crime would be me.

But I couldn't think of any alternative. It didn't seem realistic that I suddenly could turn into a desperate fugitive, this sweet Mary of a girl I'd been my whole life. Most likely, Frick and Frack would track me down and that would be the end of it. They'd put a bullet through my head and I'd be toe-tagged Jane Doe in the county morgue. The police option didn't look so bad compared to that. I was bound to get caught anyway. If I turned myself in, maybe I'd only get ten to twenty years. With time off for good behavior, I'd be somewhere in my thirties when I got out, not too late to find some guy, maybe have a family, lead a normal life again. The frozen yogurt melted to soup.

There was a phone booth outside. I flipped to L for Lawyers in the yellow pages. The heading read "See A for Attorneys". I turned to A. Most of the pages were ripped out. Made perfect sense. Thieves need attorneys. Four names escaped at the end of the alphabet, last one named Zimskind looked like my man. A woman behind me said, "You gonna read the whole fucking book or make a call?"

I said, "Excuse me?"

"I need to use the phone."

"So do I."

"Looks to me like you're reading the yellow pages."

I checked the woman out, tried to figure where her attitude came from. She was about my age. Jet black hair all bangs and shaved up the back of her neck. Alice in Wonderland hat, red paisley vest, black t-shirt, patched and faded blue jeans, mid-calf length Doc Martens. Six earrings of different shapes and sizes in one ear, three in the other. Nose pierced with a gold ring. A chain connected the ring in her nose to a matching ring in her ear.

She said, "You mind hurrying up? I don't wanna die of old age waiting."

I asked, "Where did you get your clothes?"

"Go back to the Valley," she said. Big insult.

"What would you do if the police wanted you for murder?" Just asking, wondered what she'd answer.

"Look, all I wanna do is use the phone." She didn't

expect this. Her feet shifted back and forth. Hold here, or try the phone down the street?

"Would you give yourself up?"

"Why you asking?" A little curious, wondered why somebody looked like me would ask a question like that.

"Maybe I need some advice."

"You want advice, call a shrink. I just wanna use the phone."

Advice enough. I dropped a quarter in the slot and dialed. It was a toll call. I was short a quarter. I stretched my hand to the woman, said, "Give me a quarter."

The way I said it, she reached automatically for her pocket, but stopped quick enough, asked, "Why?"

"Why does it look? Give me a quarter."

Sometimes it surprises me when people do what you tell them to do. The woman handed over the quarter, said, "Just don't talk all night, okay?"

The phone rang five, six times. Mom answered. Just her voice was all I wanted. I hung up, held out the receiver.

The woman stepped up to the phone, said, "I wouldn't."

"You wouldn't what?"

"Turn myself in."

"Why not?"

She grinned, "Can't fuck your boyfriend in jail."

I thought about that for a second, said, "Sounds like just the place for me."

A Motel 6 had a vacancy sign lit on Sunset Boulevard. I checked in, paid forty-six US dollars cash for a ground floor single toward the back. A sixty-something desk clerk with a disheveled stare and dark armpits told me to sign my name in the registration book. I blanked. He repeated I should sign my name. I couldn't sign my full name, Mary Alice Baker. Nina was the first name that came to me, because it was exotic, foreign sounding. I could imagine a terrorist named Nina. The sum total of my life to date would be my last name. I signed myself in as Nina Zero.

The room wasn't much, but I didn't expect the Hilton. I tossed on the bed a sack of stuff I bought on Melrose Avenue. The bottle of Jack Daniels was the first thing out of the sack. I filled up the ice bucket from the machine in the lobby, poured myself a drink. The first sip made me smile, the way it cut straight through the day's problems. I turned on the faucet, stripped while the tub filled. I threw my blouse, skirt, flats, hose into the trash. My body was pretty beat up. I examined the scrapes and bruises, worried over the seriousness of each one. The pain didn't bother me much until I stepped into the tub. The sting of hot water on ripped skin made me want to yell. I reached for the Jack Daniels. The bourbon glowed amber behind the steamed glass. I tossed it down. The great thing about bourbon is it deadens all shapes and sizes of pain. I made good use of the pint, until my body began to feel deliciously heavy and a smile floated to my lips. I settled into the tub, let the hot water strip away the layers of smoke and sweat. My old life peeled away like dead skin soaked off and washed down the drain.

When I felt relaxed, I poured a bottle of black hair coloring through my hair, turned on the television for something to do while the dye set. The channel was set to CNN. News was on. "Terror at LAX," the graphic said, dramatic music behind, like they already made a big production out of it, wanted better ratings than the other stations. A reporter stood in front of the burnt-out International Terminal, talked about the criminal investigation. He said the National Transportation Safety Board was working with the Federal Bureau of Investigation and local authorities to solve the mystery of the blast, which at latest count, and here he checked a slip of paper in his hand, was responsible for one confirmed fatality and twenty-three treated for smoke inhalation and minor injuries.

The anchorman came on. His face was serious, his voice grave. He asked, "Do they have any idea who could be behind this? Have any groups claimed responsibility?"

"I've heard, and I can't confirm this, that people

seeming to be of Middle Eastern origin were seen in the terminal shortly before the blast."

"Any reports on what they were doing there?"

"Several flights a day come and go from the Middle East. They could have been flying. No one knows yet."

"How about right-wing paramilitary groups?"

"A distinct possibility, but really, it could be anybody."

"Anybody with a bomb."

The reporter didn't treat the remark as funny. He said, "Absolutely right."

The anchorman recapped the story. Fire trucks raced across the screen, firemen mopped up after the blaze, a guy with blood on his face walked toward an ambulance. What was starting to seem like a dream was made real by television. I felt bad about what happened, didn't like to see people hurt. But there was this voice in my head said, *You did that, what you did is live on television, millions of people are watching, millions are wondering who you are and why you did it.* I flipped through the channels, saw Jay Leno talking to Goldie Hawn, Arsenio Hall grinning, Humphrey Bogart coming through a door with a gun. I was up there with the stars. Problem was, I didn't know better than anybody else why it happened.

I went back into the tub to rinse the dye out of my hair. The girl in the mirror looked older, harder. I toweled my hair dry, experimented around with the scissors, snipped a little here and there. It didn't take long to figure out it's almost impossible to cut your own hair. Then I realized it was okay if I messed up, messed up was part of the look. I left the bangs long in front, so they hung down both sides of my face just below my jaw. The natural angle of my hand cutting backward made the hair at the nape of my neck shorter than my bangs by about four inches. I checked it out in the mirror, front and back, decided the look was okay. The next half hour I tried to make it less ragged but mostly succeeded in just cutting it another inch shorter all the way around.

I refreshed my glass with a little more bourbon than was sensible, tossed it down. If I was drunk enough, I wouldn't feel a thing. I wrapped a band-aid around my left forefinger, pulled a sewing needle from a drug store bag, tested its sharpness with an exploratory jab. That discouraged me. I told myself not to be a baby about it. I stuck my finger up my nostril, positioned the needle above the first ridge of cartilage, closed my eyes, plunged it in. The needle lanced the side of my nose, pierced through the band-aid, lodged a quarter inch deep into the tip of my forefinger. My first reaction was to try and rip my finger away, which I couldn't do because it was pinned by the needle to the inside of my nose. Hurt like hell. But then I got a look at myself in the mirror, and the sight of my finger stuck up my nose hit me as funny, as things sometimes do when I've been drinking a bit, and I fell onto the floor laughing, because it was just like me to take aim at one thing and totally damage something else.

I thought of a new strategy to pierce my ears, jabbed the needle into a wedge of belt leather pressed on the other side of the lobes. My gold heart earrings, a gift from my mother at high school graduation, I replaced with twin silver hoops. I cleaned the new pierce marks with rubbing alcohol, clipped in a pair of silver skull earrings, just above the hoops. For my nose, I picked out a dagger stud. It caused me some trouble figuring how to get the backing up my nostril and onto the stud pin, then a couple of tries to get it right. One look in the mirror, I almost didn't recognise myself. With my black hair, blue eyes, dagger nose-stud and hoop and skull earrings, I looked downright dangerous.

Then I curled up under the covers, slept for ten hours.

The maid woke me at noon, knocked on the door, reminded me check-out time was up, was I planning to stay another night? I splashed cold water on my face, dried off, fumbled around for my new lipstick, a very dark purple, almost black. After that, a touch of eyeliner, mascara the same color. On the dresser was a bag of thrift-shop clothes. I emptied it on the bed, stepped into my new look. Faded black jeans, plain black t-shirt, crushed velvet gold vest, Converse canvas high tops, a black baseball cap embroidered in gold and studded with tiny round mirrors.

I examined myself in the full-length mirror on the bathroom door. It always seemed to me Los Angeles was about being somebody you weren't to begin with but maybe could be with a little work and a lucky break or two. People drifted here from all over the world to change who they were. I was no different. I searched the reflection for old signs of my self. Only my eyes looked the same, centered in a new face. I didn't know who I was anymore. The clues were somewhere in the mirror image of the strange woman staring back at me.

It was a long shot the police would get to the Motel 6, but the clerk saw me go in one hair color, out another, might put something together better left apart. Hollywood was sleazy, mostly about cheap fun with drugs and sex, the more I looked at it, the more I realized it wasn't my scene at all. If I was going to be smart, I needed to put some distance between my old and new identities. I figured I'd drive out to the beach, watch the waves and think about what to do next. Assumed if I got on a big enough street it would take me to a freeway and the freeway to the beach, but the streets took me to this urban-industrial wasteland on the fringe of downtown LA. I got hungrier and hungrier while I drove, passed a dozen restaurants made my stomach turn just to look at. Somewhere in a maze of side streets I passed a restaurant called Gorky's. It looked all right on the outside, better than Denny's anyway. I could get something to eat, ask directions. I parked my car where I could keep an eye on it, went inside.

Gorky's wasn't a normal restaurant, I could tell the moment I walked in. The people in it looked kind of scraggly. Every other guy in the joint had a goatee, the guys who didn't have a goatee had a tattoo showing, and some had both. The women wore hippie clothes, combat boots, didn't comb their hair. They had about as many tattoos as the guys. I almost turned around and walked out the people were so weird looking, until I remembered I was weird looking too.

There was a bulletin board for people to post stuff just inside the door. In among the various advertisements of things for sale was a hand-scrawled note somebody wanted a room-mate. That was interesting because the room was cheap and I needed a cheap room. I went to the phones around back, gave the number a call, but all I got was an answering machine didn't give any names or anything, just played a few bars of scratchy jazz and beeped. There wasn't any way I could leave a dependable message about how to get in touch with me, so I just said I was calling about the room, I'd be the one in the baseball cap hanging out at Gorky's.

I grabbed a green salad at the buffet, a bowl of borscht, meatloaf, a slice of peach pie and black coffee, paid for it at the cash register, was lucky enough to nab a table by the front window just as a party of four was getting up. After I stuffed every last bite down my throat, I stared out the window, felt lost, wondered if I should get back in the car, try to find the ocean. It was only half a million square miles big and blue in color, I shouldn't have too much trouble finding it. But the food was sitting heavy in my stomach, I didn't want to go driving again just yet. I left my baseball cap to save the table, walked out to get my portfolio and camera bag.

First thing I noticed walking up to the Honda was my right tail-light was broken. Not just broken, shot out, a big hole in the metal plate behind the shattered plastic. Bastards could have killed me. There were two shots I remembered, and found the second hole in the space between the back bumper and the hatch.

When I got back inside Gorky's, there was a bizarre looking woman sitting at my table. She was drinking a cup of coffee, smoked a Kool cigarette, flicked the ashes into the saucer under her cup. Her eyes were the bulging kind, looked like they were about to pop out of her head. Her hair was stringy and greasy. She was skinny. Didn't wear any shoes. Her feet were black with dirt. She curled one foot up under her butt and the other went sole down on the front edge of her chair. I couldn't help notice she didn't wear panties, a fact plainly visible from the way she sat and the shortness of her lime green dress. But she didn't sit there conscious of what she was doing. She didn't care so much, she didn't know. My first impression, this was either a lunatic or dirty saint.

I said, "I was sitting here before."

She didn't so much as look at me. I was suddenly unsure what the hip etiquette was in a place like this, asked, "So do you mind if I sit here again?"

Her eyes fixed on my hat. She said, "That depends."

"On what?"

"On how long ago you were sitting here. Was it a couple of minutes ago, an hour ago, days ago, or maybe you're one of those reincarnation nuts and you think you sat here in a previous lifetime."

I pointed to my hat, said it was just a couple minutes I'd been gone, see, there's the hat I left.

She looked at me very critically, said, "I was wondering what kind of person would wear a hat like that."

"What's wrong with the hat?"

"It's decorated with little mirrors."

"That's bad?"

"They look like eyes, staring at me."

I took out my camera, because the woman's weirdness inspired me. People usually think the beautiful is photogenic, but for me, it's the ugly, strange, violent. The beautiful depict what we want, but the ugly portray who we are. The first shot I took the woman stared off camera, ignored me while she smoked. The second shot she vamped, cigarette smoldering out the corner of her mouth, lips pursed and hand poised on the back of her head, big eyes rolling back in their sockets so only the bloodshot whites showed. The beauty queen pose and lack of attention to beauty in her person was wonderful, grotesque. Her irises slid back to horizontal, stared at me cynical as a clown long ago lost heart, performs with contempt for herself and the audience. I shot that, too.

Outside the window, a police car stopped on the street, blocked my Honda. Two policemen got out and walked into Gorky's. Lots of cops worked downtown, some came in every now and then for coffee and pie. But I didn't reason it out just then. I was scared as hell. I hid behind my camera. The two policemen approached the manager, hitched up their belts, adjusted their nightsticks. One of them said something. The manager shook his head. I swung my camera over to the woman. She bolted from her chair so fast I lost her out the side of the frame. I picked up her image again outside the window, standing in the middle of the street and looking toward the sky, east and west as though she searched for something up there.

The policemen finished talking to the manager, walked back out to their car. One of them noticed the woman, followed the direction of her gaze up into the sky, but whatever she was seeing escaped him. He looked at her like there was something wrong with her mind. His mouth moved, said something like, "Hey, get out of the street." The woman didn't seem to want to move, but she obeyed orders, stepped onto the sidewalk. Once the police car turned the corner, she ran into the street again, searched the sky another minute before coming back to the table.

I looked at my hands. They shook. I asked the woman for a cigarette. I didn't smoke but wanted to start. She pulled one out of her pack, stuck it in the corner of her mouth and lit it, said, "You work for *them*, don't you?"

"The police? No way."

"Not the police," she objected, like I was stupid. "*Them*."

"Which them do you mean?"

"The FBI, CIA, Mafia, JFK Assassination Conspiracy, Secret World Government, or the Alliance of Intergalactic Evil Nations, otherwise known as ALIEN. They're all the same."

The FBI was a safe bet. I said, "I don't work for them. They're after me."

She didn't seem surprised, said, "You too? Of course, that's what they all say when they want to get your confidence."

"They tried to shoot me. I got two bullet holes in my car to prove it."

"Easily faked."

She smoked, watched me. I watched back. She whispered, "Have you seen the miniature radio-controlled flying saucers?"

I said, "God help me if I start seeing flying saucers."

"God help us all. They have them now. It's how they watch us. Powered by batteries that never go dead, same technology Standard Oil bought up and concealed years ago to keep battery-powered cars off the market."

"That what you were looking for outside, flying saucers?"

She nodded, slow and solemn.

I asked, "How do you know these things?"

"I'm a film-maker. It's my job to know."

"You mean you make movies, like *Terminator*, *True Lies*?"

"I don't make Hollywood movies," she said, sneering when she said "Hollywood".

"Why not?"

"Too many people watch them."

I left the table to get a refill of coffee. She gave me her cup to get her one too. When I got back, she had opened my portfolio, was flipping through it. She asked, "These pictures yours?"

It embarrassed me to have her look, didn't show my photographs to anybody. Didn't think anybody saw the same way I did. The portfolio was half full, mostly pictures of my family I shot over the past year. Granny Faye. Pop drinking beer, fixing his pick-up. Mom cleaning house. Ray watching Mom, sitting next to Pop. I shot black and white with my family, deliberately underexposing the film and pushing it in the lab, to enhance the patterns of grain. Technically, the photographs were rough, like if you took sandpaper to the image. My family complained about it, said I made them look ugly. It was just the way I saw them, imperfectly focused, dark here and washed out there, fused together by shards of grain.

I reached for the portfolio, said, "I don't want to show these to anybody yet."

She wouldn't let me take it back, pulled out a shot of my grandmother, turned it around a couple of times, asked, "What's this?"

It was a photograph of Granny Faye lying in bed. I took it one morning after a difficult night at the rest home, where she'd lived the last couple years. I'd stayed since the afternoon before, fell asleep in the chair at the foot of her bed. When I woke, she had a look on her face not exactly peaceful but somehow beyond pain. I photographed her face blending with the white pillow, the morning sun lighting up the window behind her. It was the best way I had of understanding what happened.

"It's a picture of my grandmother."

The woman said, "She looks dead."

I answered, "I guess she was."

"That's cold. Really cold. I've never heard anything so heartless in my life. Your own grandmother. Did you call the doctor?"

"Well, she was already dead."

"That's so cold it's brilliant."

I looked at her, like, "What?"

"Can't be sentimental. Truth is brutal." The woman stuffed the photographs under the rear flap, pushed the portfolio across the table, asked, "How much can you pay?"

"You want me to pay you for looking at my photographs?"

"I was talking about rent money."

"How did you know I was looking for a place to rent?"

The woman pointed to my hat, said, "You called. Baseball-style hat, right?"

We walked to the woman's place from Gorky's. The neighborhood was all abandoned factories, warehouses, street-stripped cars. Nobody on the streets much, except the homeless. The woman said her name was Cass, she was sharing studio space with a painter named Billy b in an old ball-bearing factory just south of downtown. Cass was the one wanted a room-mate, because she was having problems making the rent. I was going to live in her half of the studio, in the room where she edited her films before the rental company came and repossessed the editing machine. My share was two hundred dollars a month, which I didn't have to worry about not having because it wasn't due until the first of the month.

Cass led me up a flight of steps, through a door with a picture of Elvis painted on it, into a painter's studio, a huge space with rough wood floors, brick walls, plasterboard partitions, ladders, open beam ceilings. A young guy sat cross-legged at the far side. Cass told me that was Billy b, the guy she shared the loft with. A cigar smoldered from his thumb and forefinger. He stared at a twelve-foot-tall painting of an eye, cheekbone and eyebrow. Some blank spots showed through here and there, where he hadn't finished painting, but even so, the eye was unmistakably Elvis. Paintings of celebrities were stacked all along the walls, up against the workbench, just about everywhere. The paintings were huge, most bigger than any wall in any place I'd ever lived. Some were complete portraits, some just famous body parts. Donald and Ivana and Marla Trump, Kim Basinger, Guns 'N' Roses, Madonna, Roseanne, Oprah, and Elvis, everywhere Elvis. The portraits were bright, hard like porcelain.

Billy b didn't move. Just sat and stared at this painting. Paint smeared his jeans and t-shirt, his baseball cap was so thickly caked I couldn't tell the original color of the cloth. Even his simple round glasses were flecked with paint. I thought he was cute, surfer boy good looks, long blond hair tied back in a pony-tail.

Cass showed me around, talked about the loft. I tried to concentrate on what she was telling me, but it was all pretty obvious, kept looking back to Billy b sitting on the floor. I was reeling from what Wrex did to me, so being attracted to another guy was on my top ten list of things not to do. But he had such gravity of concentration I was sucked into watching him. I told myself it was his relationship to the work that attracted me. I never saw anybody so concentrated in my life, the way he looked at the painting in front of him. Just when I thought maybe he wasn't real, he was a beautiful statue, he brought the cigar to his lips, said, "Doesn't work." A second later, so fast and smooth I didn't register him getting up, he stood in front of the canvas. I didn't see anything wrong with the painting. Maybe there was something he didn't like about the surface, maybe the surface was soft, when he wanted it hard and cruel. I never got close enough to find out, because he took an Exacto knife from his work table, slit the canvas top to bottom in one stroke of the blade.

I walked up and asked why he did it. He cut the painting again, said, "If it doesn't work, you have to destroy it."

Cass set a six-pack of Bohemia on the floor, said I was the new room-mate. Billy b reached down to grab a beer, and on his way back up, gave me a long and serious look.

He asked, "What's your name?"

"Nina Zero."

Cass said, "She's a photographer."

"I'm a photographer," I said.

"You any good?"

"Not much."

Billy b sat on the floor, said, "Don't be modest."

"Billy b doesn't like modesty," Cass echoed.

"Modesty is for losers."

"He thinks you gotta brag if you wanna get anywhere."

"People only know what you tell them. If you tell them your work is shit, that's what they know about you. If you say your work is brilliant, that's what they'll believe."

I listened that night to Cass and Billy b argue about art and living the life of an artist. Half the stuff I didn't understand, but listened in awe to the amount and ferocity of it. Cass and Billy b fought over aesthetic theories, philosophies, and movements I didn't know existed, never knew could be the source of such violent feeling. Words like kitsch, conceptual art and post-modernism were shouted like it was life and death they were talking about. Most of what they said had to do with something they called anti-art, which seemed to be art at the same time it wasn't. It was art with all the art removed so anybody could make it, except nobody could really understand or like it except the artists who were making it and the critics who wrote about it after. So it was like this joke everybody took real serious at the same time.

Listening to them argue, I had the same sense of anxiety I used to get in class when I was afraid the teacher was going to call on me to answer a question on something I knew nothing about. But the longer I listened, the more I realized they weren't interested in what I had to say. They wanted me to listen to what they had to say. So I did. They went on to argue until two in the morning, when they got violent about something called deconstructionism, demanded to know how I stood. By then it was easy. I just repeated a little of what both were talking about. "See, she understands," Cass said, and Billy b answered, "My point, my point exactly," and they both went back to arguing like I hadn't said anything, didn't even notice when I said I was tired and got up to go to bed.

Bed was a six-inch-thick sheet of foam, a blanket, a pillow. I shut my eyes, didn't get anywhere near sleep, every time I opened my eyes I saw the black case standing in the corner. The loft had twenty-foot ceilings, my room was built like an elevator shaft, it wasn't easy going to sleep with them arguing outside my door. So I stood, paced the room, bumped into the case every other turn. The Pandora urge to open the thing was strong. I walked around the thing, studied it. There was a lock on the side, three latches. I hunted around for the key, found it under a swatch of black tape stuck to the back of the case. The case weighed about two hundred pounds. Two hundred pounds of cocaine had to be worth about a billion dollars. I freed the key, stuck it into the lock, didn't turn it. Not that I wasn't curious. I was curious as hell, scared as much as curious.

I sat back down on the bed, tried to stare the thing down. Personally, I think Pandora got a bum rap. I read about this. She didn't put all the evils of the world in a box. Zeus did. There weren't any warning signs on the box, either. Here she was, the first woman ever created, the Greek edition of Eve—who you may notice also got a bum rap—sent by Zeus to marry a guy she'd never met before. How was she to know Zeus wanted to punish the human race because Prometheus stole fire from heaven? She hadn't even been born when that happened. I mean, of course she opened the box. It was a wedding gift from Zeus. She would have been fried by a lightning bolt if she tried to send it back. The box was a set-up job from start to finish.

I gave the key a turn and sprung the lid. Whatever it was, somebody had packed it up good. The lid opened to a wooden crate. The crate was nailed shut and stamped with that kind of writing the Russians use. I hunted around for a crowbar in Billy b's studio, found a hammer, used the nail-puller to pry it open. The crate was packed with shredded newspaper. I scooped the paper out, uncovered the corner of something white and hard, couldn't figure out what it was. It had some kind of ridge which I grabbed onto, pulled it up out of the crate, stared at it, turned it around, let it gently back down again. Clear enough what it was, though I hadn't ever seen a Russian one before, was surprised it didn't look so different. Porcelain, bowl-shaped with a hole at the bottom. New and sparkling white. A kitchen sink.

I thought, first the bomb in the briefcase, now this, a couple practical jokers, these guys deserve each other. An envelope was taped inside the lid of the case. I ripped it open. A note and key dropped out. The note was addressed to somebody named Fleischer. Said the real thing was hidden someplace the key unlocked. If Fleischer lived up to his end of the deal, he'd be given the address. Right away I knew I was screwed. Whatever was supposed to be in the case was probably stolen. The guy who stole it was trying to sell it to somebody else. He thought up this trick to protect himself in case his buyers tried to double-cross him but didn't figure the double-cross would be murder. I was the only person left alive who knew about the trick. Frick and Frack saw me take the case. No way they could know the case contained a joke. They had to figure I had the real thing, whatever the real thing was. I could show them the note, but the note wasn't even signed. They'd just say I made it up, stole the thing for myself.

I repacked the sink, just like I'd found it, closed the case. It was quiet out in the loft. I didn't know what to do. I didn't know how I could get back to my regular life even if I wanted to. I walked into Cass's studio. The lights were off, she was asleep. The phone was in the corner. I pulled the line into the kitchen, called the police. It seemed like it rang forever. Then the operator came on.

I said, "I have information about the airport bombing."

She switched me over to some guy sounded half-awake.

He said, "Name, please."

"This is what you call an anonymous tip. But I know who did it."

"Okay then, who did it?"

"Two guys with mustaches."

"These guys have names?"

"Of course they have names. Only problem is, I don't know what."

"No problem at all. We'll arrest every man with hair

on his lip, then you can come down and identify for us, okay?"

He said that real sweet, like I wasn't supposed to know he was being sarcastic. I said, "They're both about forty, drive a tan Chevy Caprice."

"License number?"

"Don't know."

"Didn't think you would."

"I know they did it."

"Can you tell me why you suspect these men?"

"Can't tell you that, no."

I heard a long and tired sigh on the other end of the line.

He said, "Thank you very much for the information."

"Wait. You got a name?"

"Sergeant Martinez."

I said, "I saw them do it. I'm a witness to the whole thing. But my life's in danger, I can't talk right now. You'll hear from me later. I'll identify myself as Madame Zero."

Then I hung up. The guy probably thought I was nuts, but if I came up with some information, he'd remember who I was. I let myself out of the loft, circled the building to the back alley, made a pile of my driver's license and credit cards, everything in my wallet that could identify me as Mary Baker. I sprinkled on some lighter fluid, struck a match. The pile went up in a spurt of flame. Plastic melted, paper blackened and turned to twisted ash. Billy b was right. If it doesn't work, you can't be sentimental, you have to destroy it.

7

I took the key in the envelope that came with the case to a place called Lieberman's Locksmith Shop, asked the man behind the counter, "You have any idea what this key is to?"

The guy was about seventy, had a sweet smile and tufts of gray hair growing out his ears. Must have been Lieberman himself. He positioned the key under a strong desk lamp, peered through the bottom half of his bifocals, said, "Unless I miss my guess, young lady, this key is to a lock."

"You couldn't maybe guess what kind of lock?"

"I could guess, but a needle in a haystack I could guess just as good."

"An old lock, a new lock, a house lock, an office lock?"

"It's from a Yale lock, that I can tell you for sure."

He motioned me to look under the light.

"See, says so right here. Yale."

He handed back the key.

"You wouldn't want to rob anybody with this key, nice girl like you?"

I was shocked, said, "No way!"

"I didn't think so, but this town, you never know for sure."

I lied, was surprised how easy it was, said, "You know how you sometimes find a key in your drawer you don't know what it goes to?"

As I was walking to the door, he called out, "Could be a portable lock, something a nice girl like you would buy in a hardware store, might put on a garage or a storage locker."

That narrowed the odds to about a million to one.

I drove away, wondered how detectives found out these things. I didn't know if there was some special school told them what to do, or maybe it was all job experience. I didn't have any experience. Didn't know what to do next. Spent the next couple days hanging out around the loft, took pictures of Cass, myself, waited to get arrested. If there was some matchbook school of correspondence taught detecting, I was ready to sign up.

Then Billy b said, "What say we go out for Chinese?"

I was surprised he asked, because he hadn't said much of anything to me since that first night. He'd started a new close-up portrait of Elvis, spent most of his hours painting or staring at the canvas. He didn't seem to know

I dropped into his studio a couple times every day to watch him paint. He burned when he painted, lit from the inside by an intensity I'd never seen before.

Billy b drove us a couple miles into Chinatown to a small restaurant he knew served Peking duck cheap. The restaurant looked like a cafeteria, all bright lights and formica. It was the first Chinese restaurant I'd ever been to had real Chinese people eating in it.

"How come you never take photographs of me?" Billy b said when we were eating duck.

I said, "What?"

"Am I boring? Is that it? You think I'm boring?"

I wanted to tell him I thought he was beautiful.

"I was afraid," I said.

"Afraid how?"

"I thought you'd get angry, would hurt your concentration."

"Just the opposite. I'm angry because you didn't."

"Okay," I said.

"You have a boyfriend?"

I thought about Wrex, said, "Not one I wouldn't kill if given half a chance."

"Is that normal for you? Wanting to kill your boyfriends?"

"Nothing normal about it."

"Good," he said, and picked up the check.

He took me to an art opening after dinner. It was the first thing like that I'd ever been to. A couple hundred people pressed into a series of small rooms, trying not to step on strange objects Billy b told me were conceptual art pieces. A tube of lipstick imprisoned behind the bars of a birdcage, sheets of Kleenex hung on fishing hooks, a long metal tube an intense guy with curly dark hair called a device for kissing. I laughed at that one, thought it was just what I needed next time I saw Wrex. Everybody wore black, drank white wine, seemed to be an artist or musician or writer in various stages of having or not having a career. Billy b introduced me around, said, "This is Nina Zero. Maybe you've heard about her. A photographer. Explosive new work."

When I got him alone a minute, I asked, "Why are you saying that when nobody knows me and you've never seen anything I've ever done?"

"You want to be successful, don't you?"

I wasn't sure I did but said, "Sure."

"I'm creating a buzz about you. Talent may be one per cent inspiration and ninety-nine per cent perspiration, but success is one hundred per cent promotion."

Before we left, a gallery owner came up to talk. Billy b didn't have to introduce me. The guy already knew who I was. Said he'd heard about me a while ago, was always happy to look at work from new talent. He was a funny-looking little guy dressed in bright colors, name was Bobby Easter, had a gallery in Santa Monica. He gave me an appointment to see him the next day.

Suddenly I had a reputation.

"Tell me about your family," Billy b said when we got back to the loft.

"Not much to tell."

He stood at his workbench, squirted colored lines from paint tubes.

"Your mother?"

"I love her."

"Your father?"

"My Pop's alright."

He mixed the paints with a palette knife, brushed a fleshy color into Elvis's cheekbone.

"Tell me about your family," he said.

So I told him. Started with the furniture and knick-knacks. The easy-boy recliner for Pop, his garage full of work tools and hunting pictures, the .45 caliber revolver in the night-stand by the bed, his hard smell of machine oil and metal shavings. The pictures of Jesus Mom hung on the walls of the kitchen, hallway and bathroom, pictures full of beautiful forgiving and grace. The decoupage she did one Christmas, cutout pictures of the whole family pasted onto a wood board carved in the shape of a heart, varnished over with high-gloss. Her sweet-sick smell of soap and anxiety.

Billy b fell into painting to the rhythm of what I said, his brush flowing with my words, falling still when the words wouldn't come. I told him about the Lutheran Church Mom and I went to until a couple years ago when I stopped going. I talked about going to junior college and dropping out because I couldn't afford it anymore. I described how a typical night at my parents' house was early dinner and three hours of television, Mom doing the ironing and Pop falling asleep in his recliner. The arguments, I left out. I didn't say how my Pop sometimes liked to hit people. That wasn't something I wanted to talk about.

"What's your family like?" I asked.

"Rich," he said, as though that explained everything.

There was something about the way he looked at his painting that I wanted to study and remember. I went to get my camera. His studio was lit by photo-floods. I clipped a couple to his workbench, lit him at the canvas. I moved around him as he painted, took shots of his hands, his waist, his face. It was sexy, the way he moved when he painted.

I said, "Talk about your family."

He said his family lived in Malibu. His dad was a

producer with a string of action-adventure hits in the sixties and seventies. His mother was a blonde bombshell in the Jayne Mansfield and Marilyn Monroe mold, her movie career stalled by an unwanted pregnancy, meaning Billy b, and finally blown away by the generational changes of the sixties. He'd grown up calling movie stars auntie and uncle. His first experience with sex was under the expert direction of an actress living in the Hollywood Hills, an old friend of his mother's who hired him to paint on the bottom of her swimming pool a half-nude portrait of herself as a mermaid.

There was something else I wanted to be seeing from Billy b but didn't know how to ask. I decided I should just say it. That should be part of the changes I was going through as a person. Part of the new person I was becoming. If I wanted something, I should feel free to say it.

I said, "Take off your shirt."

He took off his shirt, continued to paint. Billy b had an unconscious habit of wiping his hands on the front and sides of his shirt, his chest was soon smeared with splotches of paint. I shot out the roll, loaded another. Just say it, I thought.

I said, "Take off your pants."

"Okay, cool," Billy b said, took off his pants.

I concentrated on looking through the lens. I liked

what I was shooting, a brightly lit man painting naked beneath the huge eye of Elvis. I shot through the second roll. When I pulled the camera away from my eye, out of film, he stopped being a picture I wanted to take. He was a naked man I kind of liked but didn't know too well. I ran to get him a robe.

Billy b painted another twenty minutes or so, ignored the robe but sipped at the whiskey I brought him.

He said, "You ever read Milan Kundera?"

"He's the guy they made that movie from his book, right?"

"The Unbearable Lightness of Being."

He set aside his paint brush, put on the robe, said, "Kundera once wrote something about kitsch. He said that no matter how we may despise it, kitsch belongs to the human predicament." He walked up to the painting of Elvis, diagrammed the sentence on canvas. "I'm going to paint that right here, across Elvis's face."

"Why kitsch?"

"Part of my cultural heritage."

"I thought rich people had taste."

"Think about Donald Trump and say that."

When we stopped laughing, I was aware of a moment being approached. He gave me a look, and I gave him a look back suggested if he tried I wouldn't hit him. I wanted to take Billy b inside me, surround his flesh with my flesh, in the same way that a baby wants to put a newly encountered object in her mouth. I wanted to understand him.

He kissed me very sweet at first, and I thought, okay, this is nice. Before my thoughts went from nice to now what, the kiss deepened. My head started to spin, and then he had me naked in his arms with me wondering how he got my clothes off so fast. It never occurred to me that any man could touch my body and know exactly what I was feeling, what I wanted to feel, how to get me from one to the other. It was like he plugged directly into my nervous system. He set off sparks of energy that could make me shake. I was amazed at how responsive I was when he touched me. The only time Wrex made me shake was with anger. He worked just hard enough to get me excited, so I could think yeah, he's sexy, he's good in bed, and then, bang, it's over. Sure, Wrex had a great body, but I'm sorry, even if you own a Ferrari, you're not going to win many races when you've got a nine-year-old behind the wheel.

"I'm going to paint," Billy b said after, sitting up in bed.

"You're supposed to be asleep. That's what men do after. They fall asleep."

"Sleep is boring. I'm going to paint," he said.

"Talk to me first."

"About what?"

"You decide," I answered.

He talked about painting. I didn't hear much of what he told me. The sound of his voice put me adrift, thinking about his lovemaking and how he was the most brilliant guy I'd ever met. My life had been pretty short of brilliant men up to then, so maybe that's not saying much. By the time he got up to paint again, I was asleep.

8

I woke up staring at a reclining portrait of Madonna painted on the folding screen that separated Billy b's bed from the rest of the studio. The covers on the other side of the bed were cold. Madonna was smiling, held a big black cigar in one hand, reached under her skirt with the other. I think she was supposed to be masturbating. The smell of paint was in the air, blankets, my hair, on my skin. My body was warm, heavy to move. The floor squeaked somewhere out in the studio. I rolled over, sat up, saw splotches of paint like animal tracks all over my body. The only clothing I could find around the bed was my underwear. I got up, stumbled around the partition.

Billy b worked at his canvas. He didn't look at me when I walked up. Just stared at his work, a blue-smeared paint brush between thumb and forefinger. My clothes were scattered around his workbench. I put them on. Billy b propped a cut-out stencil of the letter "H" on the canvas, brushed the interior blue. The words

NONE OF US IS A SUPERMAN ABLE TO ESCAPE KITSCH were painted in blue block letters across the close-up of Elvis's face. Billy b said, "Glad you're up, wanted you to see me sign it."

"Why?"

"Because you helped create it."

"I did?"

He dabbed black paint onto his workbench, selected a clean brush, dipped it into the paint. He said, "Something you should know."

"What?"

"Women come in, watch me paint, and they want to sleep with me. I'm lucky that way."

"You mean women like me."

"Something else. I'm not into long-term relationships."

"You're saying I shouldn't expect anything else out of this, just one night."

He shrugged, like maybe, maybe not, met the canvas with the black-coated tip of his brush.

I said, "Takes no guts to be honest the morning after."

"If you regret what happened last night, it doesn't have to happen again."

I said, "Just tell me what you want, so I don't get confused."

He stepped back from the canvas, dropped the brush into a jar of solvent, said, "That's it, it's done."

I collected my camera and portfolio, drove twenty miles south through the biggest nowhere in LA, a city with a lot of places nowhere at all. Stopped at a phone booth to call my apartment, wouldn't matter if the cops could trace my call, no one would see me. The answering machine picked up second ring. My voice came on, sounding sweet and insecure, like it was really important the caller left a message, didn't hang up on me. I punched in my access code, listened to the machine rewind. Got a lot of hang ups at first, then Wrex, sounding pissed off, saying, *Where the hell are you, god-damn can't trust anybody you trying to rip me off or what?* Then Mom, Wrex a couple more times, my boss at Hansel & Gretel's, Mom asking where I was, my boss firing me for not showing up, Mom again, asking why didn't I call her. That's the one really hurt. No way I could call, explain what happened. The last message was from Wrex, not sounding angry at all, more like desperate, begging me to be reasonable. He said, *You remember where we met, couldn't forget something like that could you? Know I couldn't ever. I'll be there tonight, six p.m., so why don't you come, bring the case, okay? Nobody knows anything*

*about you-know-what, so babe, please, just bring the goddamn
case, okay?*

Like I was supposed to get all stupid and sentimental
remembering how he tried to pick me up in the lounge
at Oak Tree Bowl, make me think he was an all right guy
after all. Don't know why they called it Oak Tree Bowl,
musta been an oak tree cut down where they built it.
Wrex used to hang out there a lot, not to bowl, to drink
beer. Sure I thought he was cute, but remembering that
first night didn't fill me with romantic nostalgia. Wrex
was trying some combination drug and beer thing that
didn't mix just right, spent half the time making unex-
pected runs to the bathroom.

I drove to Santa Monica, had an appointment with
Bobby Easter, the gallery owner I'd met at the art
opening the night before. His place was called SMART
Gallery, stood for Santa Monica ART. He was uncrating a
painting of Sharon Stone and Billy Baldwin kissing when
I walked in the door. The painting was from a scene in
some movie. It was Billy b's painting. I didn't know
Easter sold Billy b's work. Like the night before, he
dressed with lots of color. Lime green suit, canary yellow
shirt buttoned at the neck, no tie, red leather shoes,
pink-tinted eyeglasses. I waited for him to notice me.
He didn't. I coughed, stepped up, said I liked the
painting.

He looked me up and down like I was something he'd

order off a menu, said, "You're Billy b's friend, aren't you." I got the feeling he wasn't judging me so much as Billy b's taste. He was curious, the way somebody will glance over to see what the guy at the next table is eating.

He said, "Well, let's have a look."

I spread the portfolio open on the corner of the reception desk. He flipped through the pages, smiled like he thought the photographs were amusing. He wanted to know where I'd exhibited before, who bought my photographs. Collectors, he called them. I answered zero exhibits, zero collectors.

He said, "You know, I never exhibit photographers."

His mouth puckered in distaste when he said the word *photographers*. I couldn't figure why he asked me to come by if he didn't like photographs. Maybe he volunteered to see me because he sold Billy b's paintings, wanted to keep him happy. Maybe it was a set-up job. Maybe Billy b told him to say he'd heard of me, so I'd think Billy b was a big shot.

He said, "Nobody will buy these if you haven't exhibited before."

He said, "Nobody will exhibit you if you aren't in any collections."

He said, "Every gallery in town will look at this and tell you to come back when you're a little further along in your career."

I zipped up the portfolio, walked away, said, "Thanks for your time."

"Hey," he called.

I stopped.

"Talk to Barbara Whitney at LACE. She's curating a group show for emerging artists. Don't wait until tomorrow. Do it this afternoon."

I said I would, moved toward the door.

"Nina," he called.

I stopped again.

"When you're done with Billy b, come and see me. It won't hurt your reputation."

I had no idea what LACE was or where it was located, but wasn't going to tell him that. I stopped at a gas station, looked it up in the white pages. LACE stood for Los Angeles County Exhibitions.

Barbara Whitney was behind the front desk when I got there. She looked rich. Pearls curved white against gray silk. Flawless makeup. Not a single ripple disturbed the smoothly brushed surface of her hair. Only somebody with a lifetime of money could look perfect like that.

I walked up to the desk, introduced myself.

She studied my portfolio while I stared at the ceiling, the clock, the counter, nervous as hell. She took her time. It was weird watching a woman like that examine photographs. Maybe it was the *National Geographic* effect that interested her, pictures from a primitive culture, because she flipped back and forth in the book as though not quite believing what she was seeing.

"And you've never been in a show before, is that right?"

I told her no, not really.

She handed me an application, said this was the last day to file so I had to fill it out now. She'd wait. I checked boxes, filled out answers, handed the application and my portfolio over the desk.

She said, "We have over a hundred applications, you know."

I said, "So don't get my hopes up?"

She said, "Life is safer that way."

Hadn't made up my mind what I was going to do about Wrex. Decided to drive North, check out his story, didn't have the case with me so I wasn't going to do things exactly the way he wanted. Maybe he deserved at least one chance to explain what was going on, how he planned to get me out of trouble. But I wasn't going to walk up, say here I am. I wasn't stupid. I was the one delivered the briefcase blew up in the airport. I didn't plan to trust him all the way to jail or worse.

The Honda was a problem, more identifiable as Mary Baker than I was. Couldn't risk parking it in front of the bowling alley, have Wrex or somebody else know I was there. I parked it on a side street about a mile away, decided to walk up. Stuck my thumb out when I reached the main road. Never hitchhiked before, wanted to see what would happen. One of those mini pickup trucks pulled over, had big tires, custom mud flaps, extra chrome, fancy lettering on the back window said *Smokin'*. One look at the guy inside, I knew he meant the lettering more than one way. Long-haired headbanger about seventeen years old, listened to Anthrax full blast on his stereo, said his name was Phil. Looked at me like I'd just made his day, asked, "Where you going?"

I told him I was going bowling. He didn't expect to hear that, I could tell he was suddenly asking himself if maybe bowling was hipper than he thought. Here I was, obviously not from around there, an older woman, exotic looking, probably someone he'd fantasize about. Bowling must be the new thing. I noticed his hand shook a little when he tried to light a cigarette, like I made him nervous. It was strange coming back to my town the kind of person seemed exotic, dangerous to the people I once lived with. Then I asked if he wanted to come with me, because I thought someone like Phil might be good cover, help me scout things out.

Phil said sure he'd go bowling, goes bowling all the time, cool sport. He chirped the tires pulling away, thought he'd impress me with his driving skills, drove with his left elbow hanging out the window, his right wrist draped over the wheel. He drove the way guys do in small California towns, real fast and then cruising slow, showing off. Dumb way to drive, but I didn't tell him that, I just smiled when he looked over to see if I realized how cool he was, pretended to gasp when he whipped the wheel left and bounced the mini-truck into the parking lot. Sure, Phil was just what I needed. I used him like a screen when I went in, nobody expected me to come with somebody, nobody expected me to look the way I did, I half-hid behind him as we went straight for the bowling lanes. We stopped at an empty lane across from the lounge. Phil set his smokes and keys on the scoring table, walked up to the counter to get shoes and a scorecard. I went up to the racks like I was looking around for a bowling ball. Wrex was sitting at the bar, turned around to watch some sports thing on the big-screen TV. Then I saw something else looked familiar, back turned at the phones like he was making a call. Rayon windbreaker and stay-pressed slacks, a guy spreading out in middle age, losing his hair. I looked around for his brother, didn't see him, didn't mean he wasn't around, waiting for me to show up. Made it seem like a trap they wanted me to walk into, was thinking I might get Phil to take a message to Wrex, when somebody started shouting in the bar.

Frick jogged away from the phones, knocked on the men's room door, his brother came running out hand dipped inside his coat like he had something in there could shoot somebody. They ran into the bar, stopped. The somebody doing the shouting was Wrex. The brothers turned to see what he was shouting about. A news bulletin. My face, bigger than life on the big screen TV. The newscaster said, . . . *twenty-four years of age, with fair hair and complexion, last seen driving a late-model red Honda Civic. Anybody with information should please* . . . The picture was from my high-school yearbook, where my blonde hair is piled high on my head in a disastrous bun, eyes unfocused, mouth gaping in a sweet but insecure smile. My vanity was offended. Here I was, infamous, and they had to broadcast the worst picture they could find.

I went back to the scorer's table, slipped the keys to the mini-truck off Phil's key chain, left a note saying I went to pee, walked out the door into the parking lot. I didn't feel good tricking Phil like that, but I was sure he wouldn't mind lending me his truck if I coulda told him the trouble I was in. I didn't know when I could give it back either, because it looked like I was going to have to borrow it permanent.

The mini-truck started right up, I popped the clutch and punched the accelerator, didn't realize how light the thing was in back, almost spun a three-sixty just getting out of the parking lot. It had a 4.0 liter V-6 under the hood, in a small car like that a big engine is like strapping a rocket to a bicycle. Second gear, I was doing forty, wasn't even red-lining the RPMs. Phil had done some work on the engine, put new pipes in the back, the thing let out a satisfying roar when I gave it some gas. The rearview mirror said no cops, no Wrex, no Frick and Frack. I headed to the edge of town, took side streets looking for a car with dust on its windshield and current registration tags. Found one parked in front of an empty lot, looked like it was abandoned. I took the front and back plates, put one on the mini-truck, drove back to my Honda and put the second on that. I grabbed my camera bag from the Honda, threw it and the old plates on the passenger floor of the mini-truck. The driver's seat was set too far back so I reached underneath where they usually keep the lever that adjusts it, felt something there underneath the seat, pulled it out. It was a plastic baggie, had a bunch of pills inside, little white ones, a sheet of paper marked off into tiny squares, each square printed with the stuck-out-tongue logo of the Rolling Stones. Reached under again, found an envelope, opened it to three one-hundred dollar bills tucked inside. Seemed Phil had a little business venture to help him make payments on his truck. A lot of kids did that in high school, was the way most kids bought their drugs, from another kid. I was sorry for Phil, but it would be a good business lesson to lose his truck, his stash, teach him about risk.

Then I just ran. Got on the Palmdale Freeway and headed east. The sun dropped below the horizon, traffic ahead moved a good ten miles faster than the speed limit. I saw the cut off to downtown LA, didn't take it, kept going east. I didn't have a plan. Just running on the open road. Traffic thinned to a broken line. The sky poured liquid blue over the desert hills. The summer heat lifted to the cool of night. I didn't need a plan. The mini-truck loped along under the palm of my hand. All I needed was an open road.

I didn't feel good about my mom finding out. My pop, let him think his daughter is a terrorist, shake loose a few of his dead certainties about the world. But my mom, she didn't need a new source of pain in her life. I hadn't even talked to her. I owed her at least a phone call. The FBI was camped out in her living room, waiting for me to call. Mom was serving coffee, asking if they wanted something to eat, worried half to death inside. She always did her best to take care of people, family or strangers. It made her feel good to be needed, that was more important than happiness. She knew how to be unhappy. Pop needed her, in his own brutal way. Ray needed her more than anybody. She was his life, I think. But Ray couldn't talk to her. He didn't know how. I was the only one who talked to her. Now I'd messed up, was just one more pain she had to deal with.

I ran low on gas near Barstow, pulled into one of those interstate complexes with a gas station, mini-market, motel, coffee shop, bar and restaurant. It was getting near eleven, I wanted to wire up on coffee. The coffee shop was bright lights, orange vinyl booths, happy muzak. I bought a jumbo coffee to go and five Milky Way bars, asked if they had a big paper bag they could give me. I took the drugs, old license plates and Phil's headbanger tapes, put it all in the paper bag and the bag in the trash. Then it was back in the truck and the long stretch of desert between Barstow and Phoenix. The moon rose above the horizon at midnight, dusted the desert floor with a silver glow. I kept the mini-truck at a steady seventy, the right speed to eat up the miles, keep the highway patrol at bay. The moon crept up the windshield, disappeared over the roof. Around four a.m. I turned south on a desert highway that promised to take me to Tucson, from Tucson to Mexico. My headlights spotlit saguaro cacti at each curve, threw three-pronged shadows along the desert floor. I didn't see another car for miles. I didn't think about much. I watched the road and the changing colors of the sky.

The sun was up and blinding by the time I hit the outskirts of Tucson. I pulled off at a coffee shop, bought a copy of the *Arizona Daily Star*, sat down to a breakfast of bacon, eggs, toast, orange juice and coffee. The newspaper mentioned me by name on page three, but no picture.

A circular display of postcards stood by the cash register. I selected one showing a saddled jackrabbit the size of a horse. Wrote my Mom I was sorry I hadn't called, but I had to leave town in a hurry. I was in trouble because somebody played a mean trick on me. Didn't know what to do, was thinking about leaving the country. But not to worry. *Life will all come out in the wash and mimic the socks. Some disappear on mysterious paths no one can figure out, some are abandoned and alone, some find a new partner, and some stay mated for life*. A running washday joke between Mom and myself, started when I was a little girl helping out, turned into a big soap opera about The Life of Socks. I knew the FBI would be reading her mail. Let them try to figure out what it meant. My Mom would understand. Life is not always predictable. I wrote I loved her six times in small print with big exclamation points, signed my name, put the card in the post box outside.

It was short of nine a.m. and the truck was already hot as a furnace. Not a cloud in the bleached blue sky. I decided I'd keep driving east, into New Mexico. I didn't know what I'd do once I got there. Get a job washing dishes maybe, keep driving, move from here to there. I didn't know anybody, didn't have any place I could go, no place to hide, the only other thing I could think of doing was buying gas until I ran out of money, driving until I ran out of gas. Once running, there was nothing to do but keep running.

A couple hours out of Tucson, I had to stop, get some sleep, didn't want to risk a motel, figured the police would keep an eye on every motel near the interstate. I took a highway south, pulled off the road where the land looked empty of people. Phil had a blanket stashed behind the seat. I tucked it under my arm and walked into the desert. A hill and outcrop of rock looked a good ten-minute hike distant, I hoped I might find a cool spot in the rocks. The desert was hot and quiet, but there was life everywhere around, waiting out the sun. Ants on the ground, birds in the spidery branches of these trees with bark almost black. Cactus shaped like pears stacked one on top of another, others shaped like barrels, or little fingers full of stickers and everywhere the saguaro, those big ones look like a man with his hands held up, so many in the hills around me it looked like an army coming down to surrender. When I got to the top of the hill, I climbed around the rocks until I found a flat one out of the sun, spread the blanket to get some sleep, stood to drink some of the Coke I brought before it got too warm.

Something below on the desert floor moved, caught my eye. I sat, watched for what it was. Looked like a dog, but it wasn't a dog, it was a coyote. It paced back and forth a couple hundred yards away, nose to the ground, scouting for something. Then it loped on. Even at that distance I could see a spot of red where its tongue hung out. I didn't think it saw me, people probably shot coyotes around there, not like in the national parks where one will practically steal food out of your hand. The coyote stopped, ears up, listened for something. I couldn't hear anything, just a little wind brushing against the rocks. Then it dropped his head, doubled back, excited about something. Paced back and forth around a cluster of sage brush, pawed and sniffed around the base.

Two rabbits broke free, sprinted different angles away from the brush. The coyote made his decision faster than I could see it happen, chased one rabbit, cut it off from where it wanted to go, caught it with a crisp and brutal snap of its jaws. The rabbit screamed when it was caught, I didn't know a rabbit could make a sound like that, like a person screaming, like the kind of scream I would make if something jawed the back of my neck. The coyote shook its head, broke the rabbit's neck, the scream stopped. Just like that it was over. The rabbit was alive one moment, dead the next. It ran, was caught and killed. No fun being a rabbit. No fun being hunted, caught, eaten. I went to sleep, slept through the hottest hours of the day. When I woke up, I turned around, drove back to LA.

9

The Steel Investigations office squatted above a boarded-up strip joint on Ivar Avenue in Hollywood, in a two-story crumble-bum structure on the biggest nothing street in Hollywood, which can be a pretty nothing town. The strip joint looked boarded up a couple years, cheese-cake eight-by-tens still in display cases, tasseled breasts bleached green by the sun. It took me most of the day to get around to Steel. I started with Pinkerton's, where an operative who looked more like an accountant told me I needed a license to work for them unless it was sec-retarial, and I didn't look much like Pinkerton's material anyway. ACE and Eagle Security and Nolan's Investi-gations, they all said pretty much the same thing. If I didn't have any experience, I had to go to detective school and get a certificate. I said to the guy at Nolan's, I didn't have time to go to school, who might hire me as is?

The guy thought about it, said, "Steel Investigations." He thought that was pretty funny, laughed, "Tell old Ben that Pat Nolan sent you."

I went through an unmarked door next to the strip joint, walked up some stairs. The door at the top of the stairs said Steel Investigations, listed the names Ben Steel and Jerry Harper. I went ahead and opened the door. A fat guy in his mid-forties was stuffed into the chair nearest the window of a one-room office. His feet were propped on the corner of the desk. His feet were huge. One size bigger, he'd have to lace up a pair of suitcases. A brass plate said his name was Ben Steel. His head was tilted way back over the edge of his chair, his eyes were closed and he was snoring.

I cleared my throat.

The man snorted, shook his head around, said, "You can leave it on the desk here. You'll find twelve bucks on the file cabinet."

I said, "What?"

He cocked open the eye nearest me, sniffed around like he was missing something, said, "What's the matter, you so new at this you leave it down in the truck?"

"Leave what?"

He said, "My mistake, thought you were somebody else."

It took a moment to gather momentum, but with concerted shoving and pulling he hauled his bulk into an upright position. He rubbed at his jowls, smacked his lips, forced his eyes to focus long enough to take me in.

"And what may I do for you, young lady?"

"Pat Nolan said I should come see you."

His eyebrows collided for a worried moment. He said, "Those big agencies, they don't always got time for the small project, always looking to make the big buck, but me, I have a more intimate operation, no job too big or small. That's what you got, something small, like looking for a lost cat?"

"Not a cat at all, a job is what I'm looking for."

He hoisted his legs back onto the corner of the desk, said, "Shoulda known. That Nolan is a son-of-a-bitch."

I said, "I'm a hard worker and easy to get along with and I learn fast and take direction well and I really want this job."

He held his hand up, said, "You got the needle on my bullshit-detector pinned to the red."

I protested it was true, I really did want this job, no bullshit about it.

"Got any experience, any special skills?"

That threw me for a moment because I didn't know what he meant.

"You mean, can I do karate, shoot a gun, that sort of thing?"

He yawned, closed his eyes, said, "Interview's over. Sorry, but I ain't hiring."

"I know cameras and film stocks better'n almost anybody, I can take a picture of anything at any distance, I could be sitting in a car across the street from your house and get a picture of the mold at the back of your refrigerator."

He opened his eyes, asked, "You got your own equipment?"

I set my camera bag on his desk and zipped it open, listed the stuff I had with me, which wasn't much, just the Nikon, three fixed lenses, a 50-150 zoom, flash equipment, and assorted filters, batteries, cleaning stuff and film stocks. Ben's jowls lifted an inch and a half from their nest on his chest. He peered a moment inside my bag, said, "Get me a cup of coffee, would ya?"

Someone knocked on the door, came into the office behind me. Gawky young kid, carrying a pizza in one of those warming bags. Ben said, "You can leave it on the desk here. You'll find twelve bucks on the file cabinet."

The kid dropped off the pizza, picked up the cash like he knew his way around. I found a Mr Coffee Maker in the corner. The stuff in the pot had boiled down to liquid tar. I poured it into a stained brown cup with bold print read *World's Greatest Lover*. Ben fished a non-filtered Lucky out of the pack from his shirt front, lit it with a silver Zippo from his pants pocket, stared at me for half a minute.

"Why you interested in this kind of work?"

I opened my mouth to answer, but he waved his cigarette to stop me. "I know, I know, the excitement, the danger, the romance. Well, bullshit. It's about as exciting as watching dust settle on a window sill, nobody's tried to hit me in twenty years, and I'm afraid to remember the last time I got laid without paying for it."

He watched the smoke curl off the end of his cigarette, sucked on the butt and blew a gray gust toward the ceiling. "I used to be in shape, but all I do is sit around on my butt, and all my butt does is keep getting fatter, on account of I need the padding, you see?"

Ben lifted the coffee cup, grabbed one of the dozen rolls on his stomach and shook it. "All the fat on my butt, it gets lonely, so my belly, it says, *Hey, can't have a poor fat lonely butt, that ain't right*, and grows enough fat to match my butt."

I lied, told him, "You don't look that far out of shape."

"You remember that guy did nothing but eat in his room until one day he had to go outside to see his doctor, couldn't fit through the door he was so big? That's me in five years, guaranteed. You want an exciting job, this ain't it. You want a fat butt, this is the job for you."

I said, "Sign me up, the fatter the better, just please give me a job."

Ben drained the coffee from his cup, dropped the ash from his cigarette into the grounds, thought out loud. "Maybe I can find something, maybe I can't. You know anything about surveillance work?"

I said, "That's where you watch things, right?"

He looked at me like maybe I was kidding him. When he realized I wasn't, he sighed, "You're right, that's where you watch things. Drop by day after tomorrow, about nine, I'll know better if I can use you."

He opened the box, gave the pizza a sniff.

I said, "I have a question."

"Ask."

"Say you have this key, you found it like on the street or something, and you need to find out what the key goes to, how would you do it?"

"Ordinary key, or is it numbered?"

"Ordinary key."

"If it was a client situation, first thing I'd do is get the key fingerprinted to try and trace the original owner, then I'd take it down to the lab and get a microscopic analysis of the metal filings to see what kind of door it fit, then I'd have posters put up all over town showing the key and asking if anybody recognized it, and then I'd draw up a bill for a couple thousand dollars and present it to the client saying, 'God just wasn't with us this time.'"

"What if it wasn't a client situation?"

"Throw the key in the trash."

"But what if you die if you don't find out?"

Ben said, "Then you die."

Billy b was sitting on the floor in front of a blank canvas when I got in. He looked beat. Two paintings stood slashed to ribbons by his workbench. Cigar butts piled up, out of the ashtray. I walked up to him. The air was thick with paint and cigar smoke. He didn't see me standing there. I thought he was just concentrated, but then I noticed it was a kind of glazed look he had.

I said, "Hey."

He didn't answer. He stared at the canvas. His eyes were bloodshot. I went over to the slashed canvases. The paint on one was still wet. I glanced back at Billy b. He watched me like he couldn't figure what I was doing there.

I said, "You miss me?"

Dumb thing to say.

"Were you gone or something?"

"Yeah, I was gone."

"How long?"

"Just a day."

"Didn't notice."

"I'll pin a note to your forehead next time."

I went to the refrigerator for a couple beers, sat down next to him. His skin had an unhealthy gray look. The air in the studio wasn't too good. He was the kind of guy got naturally obsessive about things, I guess he hadn't moved much from his work since I left. I popped the cap for him, told him to drink up. He emptied half the beer down his throat, went back to staring at the canvas. Then he threw the bottle. The bottle struck the canvas and broke against the brick wall behind.

"Problems?" I asked.

"Who really gives a shit about Kim Basinger, Mickey Rourke, Sharon Stone? They're old. The whole fucking subject is old. Warhol was painting Elvis thirty years ago."

Cass carried a bag and video camera into the studio, sat next to me and Billy b. She held the video camera in her lap, turned it on, put the viewfinder to her eye.

I said, "What's wrong with him?"

"He thinks he's washed up."

"I thought you had a gallery, already sold your paintings."

Billy b looked at me like I didn't get it. "Doesn't matter. Being written about, getting collected by museums, that matters."

Cass said, "LA County Museum of Art passed on his paintings this morning."

"I'm a has been that never was," Billy b said.

Cass turned the camera on me, said, "You didn't come home last night."

"Didn't think anybody noticed."

"Where were you?"

"Out driving."

"Going somewhere specific?"

"The desert. That's what I do sometimes, get in my car and drive."

"I thought you were trying to escape."

"Escape? From what?"

Cass reached into her bag, tossed me yesterday's *LA Times*. My high-school graduation picture plastered the front page. She asked, "Could you explain the resemblance between you and the person in this picture?"

"Funny you should say. Looks like me, doesn't she?"

Billy b grabbed the newspaper, looked at it.

He said, "Not really. Maybe around the mouth a little."

"We get that from Granny Faye. All the kids got her mouth."

The lens made a little grinding noise as it zoomed in, tightening the frame around my face.

Cass said, "You want us to believe this is your sister?"

"Cousin, on my mom's side. Weird girl. Straight as an arrow her whole life, then one day she just snaps."

Billy b said, "The eyes too, they look like you."

The lens dropped away from my face. I took a deep breath, thought maybe I'd got away with it.

Cass asked, "Why is the hair on your arms blonde?"

"Lots of people have lighter hair on their arms."

Billy b stared at the photo, then me.

"You're saying Nina is this girl in the photo?"

Cass panned the camera to Billy b.

"You slept with her. What color is her pubic hair?"

He said, "No way. No way do I believe it."

"She's as blonde as you are, isn't she?"

I got up, walked away. Cass yelled at me to wait. I didn't. I walked into my room, collected my things. I didn't have much, just the black case. What the hell was I going to do with that?

Cass stood at the door, asked, "How did you feel when you heard you'd killed a man?"

I stared at the camera, horrified she'd ask such a thing, said, "Just give me an hour before you call the police, is all I ask."

"Who said anything about calling the police?"

"Aren't you going to?"

"I'd rather make films than talk to cops."

"But you'll go to jail. Harboring a fugitive, something like that."

"Freedom of the press. It's a free speech issue."

I walked back into the studio. Billy b still stared at the news photo. I said, "It was an accident and don't ask me how because I don't know yet, but I was the one carried that bomb into the airport."

He said, "You're a terrorist. I'm fucking a fucking terrorist."

"I'm leaving right now."

"I could go to jail because you were here."

"I didn't want to involve you like this."

"You realize, they find you here, it's front page news. I won't be able to go out for a cup of coffee without people pointing, knowing who I am. Every reporter in town will be knocking on my door, taking pictures, wanting interviews."

Cass said, "A love affair between a young kitsch painter and one of the FBI's Most Wanted, sounds like a great story to me, even *Interview* magazine would want to talk to you."

"I could paint for a hundred years, never get another break like this."

"You'd be famous."

"More famous than Jeff Koons. More famous than anybody."

I said, "I just have to get my case, then I'm gone, nobody will ever know I was here."

Billy b said, "You don't get it. I don't want you to leave."

"You don't?"

"I want you to stay here, sleep with me every night until you get caught."

"But what if I don't get caught?"

"That's just a risk I'll have to take," he said.

Next morning, Billy b said we had some business to do, drove the mini-truck across town to a block looked pretty much like the urban-industrial wasteland where we started. Street-stripped cars rusted in the sun. Bright scrawls of graffiti every place it was flat. We got out of the truck and pushed into a storefront that looked as broken down as the rest of the street. A chipped front desk stretched in front of a door leading somewhere out back. Billy b leaned on a buzzer. A young Chicano bustled up to the desk, led us through the back door into a warehouse-sized print shop I had no idea was there. Billy b said this is the shop did most of his printing work for him when he did posters and lithographs.

A guy waited for us in an office at the back. Billy b introduced him as Bob, the owner of the shop, a guy who looked just like his name, pretty much the same left to right as right to left. He and Billy b talked shop a few minutes, left me wondering why I was there when Billy b said, "A friend of mine needs a new set of papers, a driver's license, social security number."

Bob said, "Your friend want something to cash checks and show bartenders, or does she need something that can stand up to vetting?"

"A cop runs her license, it should come up clean."

"I have to buy the identity for that. Totally legit paper doesn't come cheap."

"What's your out-of-pocket?"

"About five K."

I squeaked, "No way I have that kind of money."

Billy b said, "Tell you what. Stop by my studio in a couple of weeks and pick out something you like."

Bob looked embarrassed, I thought it was because one of Billy b's paintings wasn't worth the money. But the reverse was true. Bob thought the paintings were worth more than the papers, it wasn't a fair deal to Billy b. But Billy b insisted, said half the time his dealer didn't pay him, so it wasn't such a bad deal after all. I was stunned, asked myself what his generosity was all about. Sure, he could always hide paintings he wanted to save, show Bob only second-rate work. But still it was the most generous thing anybody had ever done for me outside of my mother giving me birth, and even that I think of as a mixed gift.

Bob said, "May as well get started. This your friend?"

"Someone looks exactly like her," Billy b said.

Bob pulled a camera from his desk drawer, positioned me against a neutral blue background, triggered the flash.

With new identification, maybe I could get away with it, maybe I could escape. At least I wouldn't have to worry about getting arrested by the bartender next time I ordered a beer.

I asked, "Can I get a passport too?"

Billy b said, "What do you need a passport for?"

"Why do you think?"

Bob said, "This new paper should be so clean you can go to the post ofice and get your passport just like a regular citizen."

Billy b looked worried hearing that, like maybe he was reconsidering things, didn't want to set things up only to have me disappear on him. He said, "But it takes time to get a passport, doesn't it?"

"About a month."

"That should be fine," Billy b said.

Out in the truck, I said, "I need to get something straight. Do you want me to get arrested or not?"

"What gave you the idea I wanted you to get arrested?"

"Last night, when you said it."

"I didn't mean right away. I meant later. It's bound to happen, isn't it?"

"If I stay in the country, sure it is."

"If you don't want me to help you out, just say so."

I didn't know if he was helping me out or setting me up, but I didn't say that. I said, "It's an awful lot of money, and I'm not going to be able to repay you, maybe ever."

"If I thought about the money, I wouldn't give anything away. I like you. I give paintings to people I like. But you don't need a painting as much as a new identity, so I gave your painting to Bob, you understand?"

I said, "What do you mean, you like me?"

"Just that. You're smart, sexy, and dangerous. Great combination in a woman."

"And I'll make you famous."

He said, "That in particular is what makes you irresistible."

11

I opened the door to Steel Investigations the next morning to a guy in his late twenties, all lean six feet of him dressed in denim, booted in Tony Lama lizard skin. He leaned against the file cabinet, gave me a sultry look. I looked back. He said, "It's a little early for Hallowe'en, you must be that girl Ben was talking about."

I immediately hated him and at the same time wanted to kiss him. His mouth was beautiful, the lips almost feminine in red fullness. He had a long face with a strong jaw and dark, hunting eyes. It was an Elvis kind of face, a face cruel and sensual and vulnerable in a single glance.

I asked him where was Ben.

He said, "Ben likes to sleep, so I expect he's in bed."

"You mind if I wait until he shows?"

"Yeah, I mind. I'm supposed to get you trained today. Name's Jerry Harper."

"You mean I've got a job?"

"Temp surveillance gig. Pays you six bucks an hour

under the table, keep your own time sheet. Don't cheat me so much I gotta catch you."

I said, "I don't cheat."

Jerry said, "Everybody cheats. Primate nature."

Out on the street, Jerry took one look at my wheels, said like he knew everything, "Boyfriend's truck?"

I could see why he'd think the mini-truck wasn't mine, it wasn't the kind of car a woman would drive, with its big tires, custom chrome and smoked windows, it was a boy-car, boastful and dangerous. I knew a dozen boys with trucks like Phil's, but not one girl. Me, I drove a Honda, safe and practical, but the more I drove the mini-truck, the more it got to me. The power, the flash, the speed. Sure, Jerry was right, it wasn't my car, but I resented the way he said it, like maybe I wasn't up to driving a truck like that, so I said, "My truck. Got a problem with that?"

He said, "No problem at all," said it with a grin. He hopped into a dusty gray Ford Econoline van, told me to follow, listed an address in Hollywood Hills where we'd meet if I couldn't keep up. The moment I turned my back the van launched away from the curb in a plume of tire smoke. Seemed Jerry meant for me not to keep up. I bolted into the mini-truck, fired it up, jumped on the gas pedal. The V-6 snapped my head against the rear glass, the rear-wheel torque started to slide the back-end out, I kept the gas pinned to the floor, whipped the wheel against the skid, straightened that truck right out. A yellow traffic light at Sunset caught me a hundred yards behind with Jerry flying right through it. I swung over to the right-hand lane, turned right, jetted through two lanes of fast-moving traffic, hung a suicide left into a convenience store parking lot, cut through the parking slots and scraped the back bumper on the sidewalk bouncing right onto Sunset again. I made the light at Hollywood six cars behind the van. Jerry didn't even know I was there. He turned right at Franklin, lumbered toward the hills. I pulled parallel to him at the next light. Didn't cut him so much as a look. When the light changed he tried to bust loose. But no way with him driving a van. I hung a couple of car lengths back, went with him. He gunned it up into Hollywood Hills, the van rolling through the narrow streets and twisting around fish-hook curves like an asphalt whale. The Hollywood sign loomed in the soft brown scrub hill above us. The van raced up a steep incline, gasped for air, pulled to the curb.

I slid in behind him, walked up to the passenger window. Jerry pretended to be interested in the view out his side mirror. I hopped into the passenger seat. He cruised around the corner and parked. I checked out the inside of his van. The back was a mini-office. Fax, phone, refrigerator, reading lamp, motion fan, CD Walkman, headphones, skinny futon. Posters plastered the van walls. A red 1957 convertible Stingray, a Harley with a babe on it, Miss Bud 1994. Jerry was so much like some guys I knew back home it spooked me. He told me to look out the rear window. The glass was one-way. He could look out, but nobody could see in, a little like Jerry himself.

He said, "You drive pretty good, for a girl."

I said, "Looks like I drive a helluva lot better'n you."

"I was just testing you a little. You can't fool me, you know."

"Fool you how?"

"You can dress up however you want, I still know who you are, knew who you were the moment I set eyes on you."

"Who am I?"

"You grew up in some hick California town. Your dad works in a factory or lumber mill, same thing. Your mom has a job in a coffee shop, wears a name tag on her right boob reads Marge or Betty. The kind of town all the kids go to the local park weekend nights to get high and fuck around because there's nothing else to do. You were lucky or smart or just cold, didn't get pregnant by the time you were eighteen, when you were old enough to realize there was nothing to keep you there anymore."

Jerry knew everything about me, knew me like only

another small-town kid would. The way he acted, it was his job to know. Dumb idea this was, going to work with detectives.

I said, "Where you from?"

"Up north."

"Where up north?"

"Near San Francisco."

"You mean like Novato, Petaluma?"

"Not that far north."

I thought of all the unglamorous towns near San Francisco where a young guy in LA wouldn't want to be from, would want to escape the moment he could. Somewhere not north or south, east or west, somewhere not much of anywhere. I said, "Stockton."

"Good guess."

He looked at me, his eyes climbing up my body so slow I could feel the pitons and rock hammers anchoring in my flesh. He said, "You know, you'd be pretty cute if it wasn't for that pig-sticker in your nose."

Like I should take it for a compliment.

I said, "You'd be pretty smart if it wasn't for the lump of dirt you got for brains."

His laugh brayed around the tin-can insides of the van. With guys like Jerry, you can't take any shit, not even on the first day, not even if they're your boss, because if you do, you'll have to take it for the rest of your life. He grabbed an eight-by-eleven manila envelope from behind the driver's seat, said he thought he was gonna like me. He dropped the envelope on my lap. I yanked out an eight-by-ten glossy of an actress type, what they call a head shot in the Hollywood biz. I liked Jerry, too. Liked him and hated him, same as all the small-town bad boys with nothing to live for except cheesy bravado stolen from rock stars and bad movies.

Jerry said, "Recognize her?"

I said I didn't, asked who she was. He told me her name, said she played the dumb blonde teenage daughter on a hit sitcom. Then it clicked, seeing her face on TV one night, hearing Wrex laugh and say it was his favorite show. I'll call her Alice. Jerry told me a story about how Alice was out clubbing one night, had too much to drink, slept the night with a guy she'd never seen before. This Joe sold ties at Saks Fifth Avenue, so you get the idea he was stylish but playing out of his league, like a high school ballplayer getting a one-night stand in the majors. Everything should be cool, the average good-looking Joe walks home with a starlet one night. "Fantasy fuck come true," as Jerry put it. But this Joe doesn't take it that way. The experience changes his life. He calls her the next day. She doesn't return his call. He calls once a day every day for the next week. She never answers. She never calls him back.

He falls into a weird obsession. He can't go back to being the Joe who sells ties at Saks, not now, not after glimpsing his true station in life, as consort to the stars. It's pretty harmless at first. He researches her career. Buys, steals or copies every scrap of print, film and video she ever appeared in. He wallpapers his apartment with her face. Writes her rambling letters, which, read in order, document the unraveling of his sanity. His dead seriousness comes clear when he quits his job. He tells his boss at Saks he doesn't have to work any more because he's going to be Alice's personal manager. He delivers this news with blatant hints they're sleeping together regularly and ecstatically.

The volume of his calls increases to several a day. His messages are confessions of love, worship and adoration. She needs to have someone take care of her, someone like him. No. Him exactly. He pours his heart into her answering machine in thirty-second increments until the tape expires. One day the number has been disconnected. He thinks she's been kidnapped. She's madly in love with him but can't escape. Her agent is keeping her loaded up on drugs so she'll stay away from him. Our Joe calls the agent, makes threats. He camps out across the street from Alice's house, the same house Jerry and I are watching. He's there one night when she returns home from the studio. He tries to be charming, but when he sees her the passion tumbles out in words Alice confuses for babbling. She locks herself in the house. Joe pounds on the door, pleads with her to let him in. She refuses. He says he's dying of love for her. She says she's going to call the police. Joe tries to kick down the door, but it doesn't give. He walks around to the back, hammers at the windows. The police catch him just as he's crawling into a window he shattered with his fists. His hands are bleeding. As they lead him away he calls out, "I'm dying, Alice, I'm bleeding to death for you."

The judge is understanding. Joe temporarily went off his nut. He's never been arrested before. Always been a solid Joe, a good citizen. The judge gives him a suspended sentence and restraining order that prevents him from calling Alice or her agent, from being seen within fifty yards of her house or the studio where she works, from attempting to see or talk to her anywhere on the planet.

But Joe doesn't get smart. He gets clever. Sends Alice cutout newsprint love notes under the pen name Romeo Jesus. Rents a billboard on her route from the Hills to the studios. Plasters it with a giant poster of his face, a Jesus Crucifix, and the words *I'm dying for the love of you*. Joe claims the poster is his love message to Hollywood. A number of young girls have fallen in love with his image. You see them every now and then on the corner of Franklin and Larchmont, staring up at his face in adolescent adoration. Last week, Joe mailed Alice a small glass case containing two veined and blood-red lumps of flesh that a lab identified as the hearts of two lovebirds. The police can't prove a thing, they assign Joe to the Threat Management Unit, abbreviation TMU an LA innovation in police science designed specifically to catch celebrity stalkers. The problem is, the city has so many celebrities and stalkers TMU can't watch them all, and compared to some of the other loonies Joe is considered pretty harmless.

Alice, meanwhile, is starting to get a little crazy. Thinks every helicopter fly-by is this guy buzzing her. Swears she sees him watching her with a telescope from the ridge opposite the rear deck of her hillside house. The only place she'll change clothes is in a closet. She dreams that he's coming after her with a cleaver. Wants to cut out her heart and eat it.

Jerry emptied a half dozen telephoto shots of Joe onto my lap, pointed out the color of his hair, what kind of sunglasses he favored, the make and model of his car, the address of his Glendale apartment. The first thing I noticed was Joe drove a BMW but lived in a dump. His hair was salon-cut, his complexion sun-lamp bronze. He liked to wear Polo shirts and white shorts and carry a tennis racket during the day, although it was not known he ever played a game. At night, he favored a light-blue striped blazer, off-white trousers, black loafers with tassels, went to the most exclusive restaurants in the city, sat at the bar and drank mineral water. It seemed Joe wanted to trade the shabby little façade of his life for a bigger and equally empty façade.

Jerry said, "If you see him anywhere near this place, shoot him. None of this artsy-fartsy crap either. Shoot him close enough to see his face, and make sure you get her in the shot too."

I said, "Don't you think it's a little obvious, me sitting in my car a few houses down, like maybe I should hide or something?"

Jerry said, "How long you been in this business?"

I said, "About twenty minutes."

"That's a long time."

"I was just asking."

"So much experience, you're probably thinking it's about time you took over the whole operation yourself."

"Sorry I said anything."

"Forget it. Just do your job, don't forget you don't know anything yet, don't even know who our client is."

"So who's our client?"

"Like I said, you don't know anything."

After that, Jerry considered me trained. He gave me a log book, drove me back to my truck, told me to go to work. I parked down the block from Alice's hillside house, sat in the passenger seat, watched the house in the rearview mirror like he told me to do. It was another ninety degree-plus day, second stage smog alert. Breathing was like sucking on an exhaust pipe. Nothing happened. Nobody came in or went out. I had some donuts with me in the truck, a couple cans of Coke. I began to understand what Ben meant about getting a fat butt.

Jerry came to relieve me at five, didn't say a word, just drove to the other side of the house and parked, pointed me gone with a long index finger. I drove downtown, passed a billboard advertisement for the phone company. The main character was a white girl-next-door type in shorts and rumpled college sweatshirt. A book was tucked under her arm, she held a sheet of paper had "A+" scrawled along the top. She cradled a telephone between her neck and shoulder. Her mouth gaped, her eyes were bright with excitement. The telephone line stretched to another telephone on the opposite side of the billboard, where Mom and Dad listened, surrounded by the latest appliances in a sparkling kitchen. Dad was home from the office, tie loosened, a swath of fatherly gray at his temples. A tennis racket was clenched in Mom's free hand. Her tennis whites were clean and bright as her kitchen. The top of the billboard was stamped with the slogan *Good news is as close as your telephone.*

I never saw my family depicted on billboards, in

television commercials, magazine advertisements. Was it my fault, some past-life karma thing? Why did I have a silent, absent and angry pop? And my mom, where was her chance at leisurely tennis afternoons? Why was it that our kitchen never sparkled? How come I never called home all breathless with excitement about anything? Why wasn't my family happy? I wanted my share of those perfect billboard moments of life. I wanted to think about my family with happiness, not be troubled by sadness and doubt and resentment. I wanted to come from a family with more money than problems.

I stopped at a Ralph's Supermarket, cruised the aisles for comfort foods. I loaded the cart with stuff my mom would buy for a summer dinner. Kraft macaroni and cheese, Heinz ketchup, French's mustard, Farmer John's Ballpark franks, Ralph's hotdog buns, Lays potato chips, a six-pack of Bud for the grown-ups, RC Cola for the kids. It made for some kind of connection, and I felt less lonely watching the items roll toward the cash register belt. My family legacy was a taste for specific brand-name foods.

I carried everything up to the studio kitchen, went to work. I put two pots of water to boil, one for the macaroni and cheese, the other for the franks, emptied the potato chips on a platter, popped one cola for now, stored the rest in the fridge. When the macaroni was done I mixed in the powdered cheese with a wooden spoon, until the sauce was a familiar pasty yellow.

Billy b came into the kitchen for a beer, looked at the brand names scattered on the counter, said, "I didn't know you could cook kitsch."

"I grew up on it."

"I heard food like this will kill you."

"Sure will, just takes some time doing it."

He said there was a Hibachi on the roof, why don't we have a barbecue. We loaded the food on a tray, climbed the ladder through the skylight. Billy b watched me grill the hot dogs under a sky the color of curdled milk. Downtown skyscrapers towered out of the smog to the north. Tarpaper roofs, power lines, smokestacks stretched east to the horizon. A city of angles, lines, intersecting planes, the geometry of it confused me. I wished I could see it through my camera, so big and dirty it was one of the most beautiful things I'd ever seen.

Billy b dropped down into the studio for what he said would be a couple more beers, but when he returned, he had a blanket tucked under his arm, the two beers in one hand, a condom in the other. The city spilled its noise and fumes around us as we made love, our throats thick with smoke and dust, our bodies slick with sweat, our cries a drop of rain on the parched landscape, and I thought about a photograph I'd like to take from the perspective of one of the skyscraper office lights clicking on above us, of these two liquid forms making love on a tarpaper square in the geometry of the city.

When we were done, he said, "I want you to do something for me."

I said, "What?"

We got dressed and climbed down to the studio. Billy b picked up a sack, carried it to his workbench. I followed him. He took me by the shoulders, walked me to a spot a couple feet to the side of a blank canvas propped against the wall.

He said, "Stand here," looked me up and down like I was a mannequin. A broom leaned against the corner of the studio. He snatched it up and tossed it to me.

I said, "You want me to sweep the floor?"

"Pretend it's a gun."

He put the viewfinder of a Polaroid camera to his eye. I forgot to look away. The flash almost blinded me.

He said, "More aggressive."

"But I don't know anything about guns."

"Pretend."

I put the broom under my arm, like it was a machine gun.

"Good, now make your eyes hard, like you're about to shoot somebody."

I squinted.

"Do something with your mouth."

I curled my upper lip, felt stupid.

The flash seared my image into the emulsion. The camera spat film into Billy b's hand. He watched the chemical haze burn away, taped the photograph to the upper corner of his canvas.

I said, "What are we doing?"

He reached into the sack on his workbench.

"I always work from photographs."

"You're going to paint me?"

He shook the sack bottom up. Out spilled a dozen pink roses, a blonde wig not too far different from my original shade. He tossed the wig so I could catch it.

"Before and after. The girl next door turned mad killer."

I fit the wig over my head, said, "I have a problem with the mad killer part."

"Think of it as iconography."

"It'll be my face. People will think it's me."

"People will think what I tell them to think. It's not you. It's the media-crazy process of fame, of becoming famous in America. The media storm is brewing over our heads, you're the one standing higher than anybody else, giving the finger to heaven. You're about to become the lightning rod for celebrity."

"But I don't want to be famous."

"Doesn't matter. You are. Frankly, I'm jealous."

Billy b thrust the roses into my arms.

"Hold them like a baby."

I cradled the roses and smiled.

The flash sparked. I felt burned, blinded.

Billy b said, "Like it or not, for fifteen minutes you're going to become the most famous person in the world."

12

I bought a newspaper and jumbo cup of coffee at the 7-11 on Sunset, parked and read it down the street from Alice's. News coverage of the airport bombing had dropped to a small box in the lower left corner of page five, pushed back by newer and bigger disasters. The article went,

BLAST VICTIM IDENTIFIED

Los Angeles—Police identified the sole fatality of the July 10th bombing at LAX as Viktor Kabyenko, age 47. Identification had been delayed, according to the Coroner's Office, due to the fragmented nature of the remains. Police investigators theorize Mr. Kabyenko was standing at or near the epicenter of the blast. Born in Moscow, Kabyenko defected from the Soviet Union in 1982. He became a naturalized citizen in 1986 and was active in the import-export business at the time of his death.

The way I was thinking at the time, Mr Kabyenko was hardly an innocent victim. It looked to me like he made a deal with Frick and Frack for whatever was supposed to be in the case. Only Frick and Frack for one reason or another didn't want Mr Kabyenko around after he delivered it. When Jerry relieved me that afternoon, I drove to the office to talk to Ben, see if I could trick him into helping me a little.

It was about a hundred degrees in the office when I got there. Ben was wedged into the chair nearest the window. He'd taken off his shoes, his feet propped on the desk looked big as hams. His head was tilted back over the chair. His eyes were closed. He was listening to opera on a boom box, I didn't know much about opera, the cassette next to it said *La Bohème*. A dead meat smell mingled with a couple dozen cigarette butts stubbed out in a black ashtray from the Stardust Casino in Las Vegas. Two pizza boxes, family size, lay twisted near the trash can.

I turned down the boom box, said, "You keep eating and smoking this way, you'll kill yourself."

Ben peeled open an eye, said, "That's one way to lose weight, I guess."

I kicked at the pizza boxes.

"You eat both these yourself?"

"Sure did."

"That's kinda excessive, you think?"

"About normal. I'm what you call a binge eater. Sometimes I eat a whole lot. Other times, just a lot."

He pointed to a broken six-pack on top of the file cabinet.

"How about gettin' me a coke?"

The coke can was about ninety degrees. Ben chugged it in ten seconds flat, tossed the empty at the trash can. He missed by a good three feet. His lungs hacked the debris from his last cigarette, cleared it out for a fresh smoke, which he lit and dangled from his lower lip. I lifted the Nikon from my bag, looked at Ben in the changed world of the lens, trimming and shaping his image through the viewfinder.

He said, "Don't you got better things to do than annoy me?"

I snapped a shot of him, the cigarette dangling out of the corner of his mouth, his head turning away, his eyes half closed as the back of his hand flashed through the frame.

I said, "I wanna learn about the detective business."

Ben flicked an ash in the direction of the Stardust ashtray, said, "You're workin' already. What more you need to know?"

"How to find people."

"What kind of people?"

"I dunno, just people."

Ben and started to move. He rolled his legs onto the floor, moaned as though the effort might kill him. He swiveled around and pitched forward in his chair. I thought he was going all the way over, face first onto the floor, but he knew his own gravity and the chair held under him. He rummaged around behind his desk, came up with a massive three-ring binder. He held it a foot above his desk and let it drop.

"This is my missing persons book."

He flipped it open at random, waved me over.

"Whenever anybody offers a reward to bird-dog the missing, they go here into this book. Mostly it's kids they want to find, but you got people from all walks of life here. Guys went out to the store for a pack of cigarettes and never came back. Girls went hitchhiking destination nowhere. Runaways. Missing heirs and heiresses. Amnesia cases. And the biggest section of all, child-custody kidnaps."

I said, "Let's say the person isn't missing, but say, just for example, he works in import-export and you need to find out where he lives without anybody knowing you're asking."

Ben lit up, watched the smoke drift like he was thinking hard, said, "Well, if it was a client situation, I'd run a credit check, then as back up I'd get a friend of mine to look him up with the Department of Motor Vehicles, then to back up the back up I'd hire three operatives, have them work a three-man tail, follow the guy around until we knew where he lived, where he ate, if he was getting any how often he was getting it and with who, should be able to bill a couple grand that way."

I said, "You don't get much business, do you?"

"No, but what I do get I maximize."

"What would you do if it wasn't a client situation?"

Ben pointed to the white pages, said, "I'd look in the phone book."

I looked at him insulted he thought I was so stupid.

"Rule one in detective work is try the obvious first. What's the guy's name?"

"No guy at all, it was just a hypothetical."

"If I want bullshit, I'll buy a fifty-pound sack."

I thought, why not, said, "Kabyenko." Spelled it for him, too.

Ben pulled the white pages from the shelf, looked it up, asked, "Mikhail?"

"Viktor."

He dropped that book on the floor, selected another from the shelf, thumbed the pages, turned it around for me to see. "There's a Victor Kabyenko in Woodland Hills, on Ellenview."

I looked at him like, shocked, said, "That was easy!"

Ben turned the boom box up again.

I listened a few minutes, high-pitched voices, low-pitched voices, classical music in between, I just didn't get it. I said, "Hey, how come a guy like you is interested in sissy stuff like opera?"

Ben said, "Opera is the only place in the world where the hero is a fat guy who gets the girl in the end. Maybe he gets shot, stabbed or hacked to bits, but at least he gets laid."

A white convertible Rolls-Royce Corniche was parked in front of the loft when I got home. In the fading twilight, its paint glistened as pure and virginal as the creamy white hind parts of an angel. I coasted to a stop a good car-length behind the Rolls, rode the last few yards to the curb with both feet on the brake pedal I was so terrified of hitting the thing. Up the block, a warm gust of Santa Anna wind swept a sheet of newsprint down a garbaged-up gutter, lofted it over a flattened trash can, sailed it past the street-stripped Buick two doors down. The newspage, cartwheeling and skidding through the air, seemed certain to make a direct hit on the Rolls, until a last-minute shift in wind direction drifted it slightly off course, saved the Rolls from a smudge or worse.

I found out whose car it was when I walked into the studio. Billy b was talking to Bobby Easter, didn't see me come in. I went to my room. All those hard surfaces, high ceilings, sound really traveled in the loft. I sat and listened. They were talking about me. Weird experience, listening to somebody you know talk about you when they don't know you're there.

Bobby Easter said, "You mean that sweet little girl?"

"That sweet little girl is a killer," Billy b answered.

"I mean, she was right there in the gallery with me."

"And you didn't have a clue."

"She wouldn't do anything violent, would she?"

"Depends on how far she's pushed, I think."

"Define far."

"That's the one thing I don't know."

"You're calling the police, of course."

"No. I'm letting her stay."

"Suppose she tries to kill you."

"She won't."

"The cops will throw you in jail just for having a cup of coffee with a person like that."

"I should be so lucky. Think about Jeff Koons."

Jeff Koons was one of Billy b's idols. Some painter and sculptor invented kitsch as an art form. Did the kind of little dogs in ceramic my Mom would buy in a drug store, the ones with pink tongues, big eyes and bow collars, only Mom paid about a buck-fifty for hers and Koons sold his little dogs for thousands of dollars.

Bobby Easter said, "What about Jeff Koons?"

"You remember what happened to his career when he married a famous Italian porn star?"

"I get it, good publicity."

"Not just publicity. A whole new work. A series of paintings devoted to famous American criminals."

"It's one thing to have Kim Basinger on your wall, something else Charles Manson."

"Think of crime as part of consumer culture. What we're dealing with here is the entertainment business. Criminals are celebrities now, big as movie stars. It's the commercialization of bad taste in behavior. It's kitsch."

Bobby Easter said, "Yeah, but I can get a hard-on looking at Kim Basinger."

"You don't think this girl can give you a hard-on?"

"What about that hooker a year back, the Beverly Hills madam, remember her? The one arrested with all those Hollywood names in her little black book."

"Exactly what I'm talking about. Imagine walking into your gallery, and there she is, Heidi Fleisch, up on the wall bigger than life, next to that woman who cut off her husband's dick."

"Lorraine Bobbitt? Scary woman."

"Then, at the end of the gallery, screened off and alone in a small room, you walk up to this."

A noise, sounded like a big canvas being moved.

Bobby Easter said, "Kinky but still cute. It works, but from a publicity angle, it works better if you two are fucking."

"Since when do you have to worry about me not fucking someone?"

They laughed.

Easter asked, "But what if she doesn't get caught?"

Billy b said, "I'm just a painter. Publicity is your responsibility."

I lay back on the bed, waited until Bobby Easter left the studio. I got up, washed my face in the bathroom, picked up a carving knife in the kitchen, walked into Billy b's studio. He sat on a stool, stared at the painting of me. I almost softened, seeing him look at his painting. But I didn't. I walked up to him with the knife in my hand. He looked at the knife, didn't understand what I wanted with him, held his hands up, pretending I was going to stab him. I slapped the knife handle against his right palm, showed him my spine.

"You wanna stab me in the back, now's your chance."

"What are you talking about?"

I bared my neck to him.

"Maybe you'd rather slit my throat."

"You're crazy."

He tossed the knife onto his workbench.

"I'm a lunatic, a killer."

"You were here, heard Bobby talking to me."

"Not exactly. I was here, heard you talking to Bobby."

"I didn't tell Bobby any different than I told you."

"I haven't heard you tell me I was a killer before."

"That was just to get him juiced up about the new work."

"You tell him who I am just to get him excited, help you sell a few more paintings?"

Billy b looked at me like he didn't see a problem, said, "Sure."

"You just about ordered him to call the cops on me."

Billy b got up from his stool, tried to put his arm around me, said, "Why would I go to the trouble of buying you a new identity if I was going to turn you in the next day? If you think about it logically, you might see I'm trying to make it possible for you to stick around a little while, not get arrested right away."

I pushed him away, walked out the door. Funny thing is, I wasn't so much bothered by the fact he was getting ready to sell me down the river as I was his crack about fucking.

13

Close to midnight, half the cars downtown were cops prowling for drunks, the other half drunks trying to stay clear of the cops. I looked like trouble in the mini-truck, just the kind of social misfit who might drink and drive, not have insurance. I kept the speedometer five miles under the speed limit into Hollywood. I knew where Jerry would come down the Hollywood Hills onto Beechwood, parked there at a quarter to midnight. I spotted the hulking shape of his van as it sped down the hill, flashed my headlights one-two, one-two.

He drove right on by. I thought he'd missed the signal until he pulled a U-turn in the middle of Beechwood, drove past me again, this time heading up canyon. Jerry had a head for intrigue. I started the truck and followed him. The houses thinned. Roadside trees flashed silver and green in my headlights. The truck's big tires thumped from asphalt to dirt, gravel kicked against the undercarriage. The houses disappeared. The road wound into a scrub-brush canyon. My headlights picked up a horse corral and barn in the distant dark. It was crazy. Five miles from Sunset and Vine, here it was cowboy country. But that's LA From any point in the city it's always five miles from the other side of the world.

Jerry nosed the van up to the corral and cut his lights. Had a beer waiting for me when I got out of the truck, but what I had in mind that night, I asked for a coke instead. I rested my foot on the lowest rung of the split rail fence, looked at the jagged black line of the ridge against the blue-black sky. The horses stood at the opposite end of the corral. About twenty in the herd, most with Mustang blood, short and squat with blockish heads. "Whore-ses," Jerry called them, because they worked the tourist trade, would give a ride to anybody with twenty bucks. I popped the tab on my coke. The lone Pinto in the herd wandered over, the slow clop of her hoofs on dirt a dim memory of afternoons in the corral where my sister at fifteen kept an old mare about the same age.

I said, "I was just thinking tomorrow I might try to park down the hill, take my camera and go around to the back of Alice's house, maybe fool Joe into thinking nobody was watching."

"Only one thing wrong."

"What's that?"

"You're thinking again. Not that I don't think you're smart, because I'm sure you are, but like I said before, you don't know anything, and if you don't know anything, thinking can be dangerous."

"So we're kinda protecting her just by being there, is that it?"

"Sure, something like that."

I filled a cupped hand with coke, offered it across the fence. The Pinto sniffed at it. Jerry told me to be careful and I said, "No problem," because I knew the horse might get confused, give my hand a good nip. So I was careful, the Pinto was cautious, between the two of us she lipped the coke down just fine.

Jerry thought that was pretty good, I could tell by the way he grinned. He asked me, "Know how to ride?"

I told him I rode some as a girl.

"Few things sexier than a girl on a horse."

"Except maybe a boy on a horse."

"I know the people here, can get us saddled up in fifteen minutes. You take that trail up the ridge, there's a patch of open country up top, and further on, you get a view of the whole damn city, lights sparkling like stars far as you can see. The horses here know the trail so well, all we'd have to do is hang on to the pommel and offer a little encouragement."

It was about the most romantic idea I'd ever heard. At some point in the ride we'd dismount and look up at the quarter moon and the stars and let biology take its course with the same sure-footedness as our mounts on the trail.

I was angry at Billy b, but not that angry. I told Jerry he was a good guy, I liked him but I had a boyfriend. Said what a great painter Billy b was, how interesting the people he knew. Really talked up the scene. Jerry listened quietly, nodded every now and then, drank his Miller.

When I stopped talking, he said, "I was hoping you came up here tonight to talk about something a little different than your boyfriend."

"Actually, I was hoping to borrow a crowbar, maybe a flashlight if you got one."

"What do you need a crowbar for?"

"I need to break into a house."

"What's the matter, we're not paying you enough, you need to supplement your income with a little breaking and entering?"

Jerry opened the side door to his van, dug out a tool box.

I said, "It's not what you think. It's a friend's house."

"Sure, and your friend forgot to pay the electric bill, so that's why you need the flashlight."

I asked, "You know anything about alarms?"

Jerry handed me the crowbar and flashlight, said, "Sure. If you're where you shouldn't be and one goes off, you should probably leave."

Good advice. I walked back to the truck.

Jerry said, "You don't know much, do you?"

"Just enough to get arrested, probably."

"Go in through a window where nobody can see you. Look for contacts, those are little things by the window corners, if somebody opens the window, they go off. If you see one, break out the glass, crawl through without opening the frame. If you see something looks like tape around the edge of the window, that means you can't break the glass without setting off the alarm. If you see both tape and contacts, you need a glass cutter. If they have a motion detector, forget it, you won't see it until you're caught. But this is Southern California, every little earthquake sets those things off so you probably won't have to worry. Once inside, go to the closet nearest the front door, that's where they usually put the controls. If you don't see any, you're fine. Also, listen for the phone ringing, security companies usually call first to see if it's a false alarm. Got all that?"

"Sure. Why you know all this, anyway?"

"There's a whole hell of a lot about me you don't know."

I liked that and I didn't, and I liked it for reasons I shouldn't have. Just before I started the engine he leaned into the open window, said, "If you ever wanna go on that midnight ride, let me know."

Then he kissed me soft and easy on the mouth.

My headlights flashed across his lean body as I swung the mini-truck around, and he gave a little salute as I pulled away. I was surprised as hell. Not just that he kissed me. But that I wanted him to do it again.

Two a.m. in Woodland Hills, not a lot going on, a few late night liquor stores still open, a couple cars stopped at every red, not much else to do that time of night in the Valley but drive. I found Ellenview easy enough, parked the mini-truck around the corner from Kabyenko's house, stuck a crowbar and flashlight into a sack, walked through the side gate into the back yard. The house was typical suburban California. Shake roof, stucco exterior, wood trim, redwood-stake fencing around the back yard, a couple orange trees offering boughs of fruit across the fence. I sat in the patio deckchair a minute or two, listened and watched and thought about what I was going to do. When I was growing up, there were lots of houses like Kabyenko's being built on the other side of the freeway. I used to go onto the construction sites and look at the houses as they went up. I'd think about myself owning a house like that one day. When the houses were almost finished, I'd break inside, walk around the uncarpeted floors, think about where I'd put the stuff I'd own. I wanted more than anything to be middle class. Life changes you, changes your dreams.

Kabyenko had track-locks installed on the sliding glass door. Tough to beat. I checked the frame, didn't see contacts, peered inside, saw no lights, no sensors, no sign of a burglar alarm. I moved along the back wall. The window above the kitchen sink had an aluminum frame and sliding catch-lock. I wedged the tip of the crowbar into the frame and popped the lock, about as quiet as a cough. I pulled myself through the frame, slid down off the sink, closed the window behind.

It was clear somebody had been inside since Kabyenko. Things were taken out of cupboards, only half put back. I walked through the kitchen and dining room into the living room, crowbar up and ready for no reason except I was scared. The sofa and easy chair were cut, fabric folded back, stuffing pulled out in a neat pile. The stereo jutted away from the wall. The carpet looked like it had been yanked up in the corner, then laid back down. The front curtains were drawn open. The police must have been through everything. Whoever searched the place took their time, respected the sense of order.

The den was off the living room, toward the back of the house. I settled down at the desk, propped the flashlight so the beam pooled on the desk top. No dust had settled onto the surface, I noticed. Drawers were pulled half out, papers stacked off to the side. I thumbed through the stack. Mostly personal correspondence. Anything incriminating, the police would have taken as evidence. I searched the desk drawers for something the police wouldn't know about. Fleischer's name. Didn't see it. No address book or business cards. In the back of the bottom drawer, I found a lock box. Somebody had scratched around the keyhole, given up and pried the lid open. Kabyenko's expired driver's license was still inside. I stuffed the license in my back pocket.

A car drove by outside. That time of night, quiet street like Ellenview, any car was cause to worry. I clicked off the flashlight, crept on all fours to the guest bedroom. Outside, a car door slammed. I braved a glance out the window. A squad car was parked at the curb, two patrolmen coming up the front walk. I dropped to the floor, crawled into the hall, lay flat as a snake, waited. The front door rattled, I was sure it was about to come flying open, but it didn't, it held. A flashlight beam swept across the living-room carpet, over the cut sofa, up the walls. I remembered the windows, how all the curtains were pulled back. Pulled back so anybody walking around inside could be seen from the outside.

The cops talked about something as they circled the house, voices muffled by the walls. A flashlight spot-lit the side window, the gate creaked, the sliding glass door in back shook. They didn't have keys. If they had keys, they would have come inside to look around. A beam of light traced the edges of the sliding glass door. I thought about what they were doing. They were looking for signs of a break-in. Scratch marks or dents near locks. An unlocked door or window.

I tried to think if I remembered. Remembered to lock
the window. I closed it. I remembered closing it behind
me. Nothing else. I scrambled on my belly into the
kitchen, slithered up against the wall. They were just on
the other side. I could hear footsteps moving toward the
kitchen window. I was going to be late. I reached out for
the catch-lock. The footsteps stopped. One of them said
something, I couldn't hear what, a laugh got a dog
barking next yard over.

I slid the lock shut, pulled my hand away. A beam
spot-lit the window, raked across the frame. A hand shot
toward my face, rattled the glass. I eased down on my
heels. A flashlight beam played along the cupboards
opposite. I started to breathe. The beam angled sharply
down, glanced white across my knee. I jerked my knees
against the wall. The beam turned back to where my
knee had been, hovered on the floor, looked for something not there anymore.

Then the light clicked off and the footsteps scuffed
away, around the side yard, down the front walk. I
crawled to the front door, my ear up against the mail
slot. Listened to door slams, the squawk of a radio, the
squad car pulling away. I laughed, couldn't believe I
wasn't caught. My first instinct was to get out of the
house. I crawled over some old mail in the front hall
going to get my flashlight in the den. I wanted to slide
open the window, jump outside, run. The adrenaline

pumping through my system made me stupid. It was safer where I was. If it was the neighbors called in, said they saw somebody, they'd stop watching the house soon, go back to sleep. I crawled to the front door again, picked up the mail, carried it into the master bedroom. I was thinking I'd find a big closet there, but the bathroom was even better. No windows. I closed the door behind me, clicked on the flashlight.

Looked like somebody checked the mail regularly. It was mostly junk, a couple days' worth. Three neighborhood circulars, an offer of credit, a solicitation for membership in a local health club, gas, something from an airline, credit card bill. I slit open the credit card bill, read down a long list of charges. Kabyenko burned up the credit those last weeks. A couple pages' worth totaling almost ten grand. Luggage, hotels, meals, clothes.

I opened the envelope from the airline. It looked like a credit card bill. I never knew you could get a credit card specialized in airplane tickets. The statement listed two flights, St Petersburg to LA. The first charge, Kabyenko flew into LA on 2 July, flight 1071, it cost him fourteen hundred bucks round trip. He repeated the flight on 9 July, the day before I met him, was billed just over two thousand. St Petersburg was a lot of time zones away, the plane was flying west with the sun, I never was very good at math, had no idea how that would all work out in terms of time. I crawled to the phone in the den, looked up and called the airline's all-night number for flight information.

When information answered, I said, "Could you tell me what time flight 1071 from St Petersburg to Los Angeles, what time it gets into Los Angeles?"

She told me to hold a moment. I heard her fingernails clicking on a keyboard. She said, "That's flight 1071, leaving St Petersburg at 11:05 p.m., and arriving at LAX at 5:25 a.m."

"So let's say it leaves on 9 July, it arrives when?"

"It arrives in LA on 10 July."

"Are there any flights that arrive closer to noon?"

"One from Moscow arrives at 9:55, but nothing from St Petersburg."

I thanked her, hung up. I met Kabyenko a little after noon 10 July. He'd flown into the airport six hours early. Probably said he was coming from Moscow, bought himself a little extra time. Did he leave the case with the sink at the airport and hide a second case? If he hired out a storage place, maybe he'd used his credit card. I examined the statement again. No record of anything resembling a storage locker appeared on the list. He'd paid cash, or stored the thing somewhere else, maybe someplace where he worked. I looked again at the flight charges.

I called the same number, said, "I'm looking at my husband's charge statement here for a flight he took, I notice he was charged over six hundred dollars more for taking the same flight a week later. Is there some billing mistake, or maybe he flew first-class the second time?"

The operator asked for the flight number again and the amount charged, said, "No, the difference between first and coach class on that flight is five thousand eight hundred dollars."

Must be nice to be rich, pay six thousand bucks more just to stretch your legs, drink champagne.

Information asked, "Was he carrying extra baggage?"

"Why is that important?"

"All flights carry additional charges for extra bags or excess weight."

"Six hundred bucks' worth?"

"Depends on the weight and number of bags over the limit."

I hung up, climbed out the kitchen window. The air was cool, smelled fresh, I breathed it deep in my lungs, recognised the taste of flowers and earth. Another couple hours the cars would come spilling exhaust and the factories spit fumes and the sun rise hot and high to bake the air to a harsh and metallic taste. But just then I was happy to walk in the violet dark, smelling the air and thinking I knew something I didn't know before.

14

I drove the major boulevards that spoked out of Los Angeles International Airport, roads a guy looking for a place to store something close to the airport might drive. I imagined I was Kabyenko, nervous about what I was planning, knowing I'd have five hours between landing and delivery, giving me an hour to get my two cases through customs, four hours to get one hid, worried the plane would be delayed, I'd have only one or two hours to get it all done. I'd leave the case with the sink in baggage claim, be a little worried someone might beat baggage security and steal it while I was gone. When a storage facility hit me as easy to get to, secure and private, I stopped, noted the address, gave the front desk a call.

The last time, I gave my voice an anxious sound to it, like one of those people can't say anything without their voice rising at the end, "Hello? My name is Marge Kabyenko? I have a small problem I hope you can help me with? My husband, Vic, he rented a storage locker, stuck the receipt in his back pocket? I washed the pants, erased all the ink, now I don't know what was on the receipt, and Vic's out of town, I need to get into storage?"

The man said, "Sorry, but I can't let you in to any locker here unless you're registered on the rental agreement."

I said, "I don't need you to get me in, I have the key right here, I just need to know what the locker number is? My husband can't remember the darn number either, talked to him just this morning out in Dallas?"

The man said, "Last name's Kabyenko?"

I dug Kabyenko's expired license out of my back pocket, spelled it for him.

"Can you give me any identification?"

"I'm looking at his old driver's license? The number on it says California N0455886."

The man said, "That's storage locker number 558."

I drove around the corner, parked the mini-truck in the facility lot, located the door to number 558, unlocked and opened it. The case was in the corner. On the outside it looked exactly the same as the first one, except there was an envelope taped to the top of it and not inside like the first time. I tore open the envelope, found a letter and customs form. The letter said if all went as planned, Mike was reading it, goodbye and good luck. If somebody other than Mike was reading it, they should know the buyer was Mike Fleischer of Fleischer Security. I read the customs declaration, it said Kabyenko carried plumbing samples, the value less than five hundred dollars. This Kabyenko guy was full of good jokes. I figured he brought two cases from St Petersburg, listed them as plumbing supplies, put a sink in one case, something considerably more valuable in the second.

I sprung the latches, saw crating like before, stenciled with that Russian writing, took the crowbar and pried it open. Shredded paper packed the case, different kind of paper from before, not newspaper but butcher paper. The object was held in place by wood blocks carved to shape. I reached inside, pulled out the paper shreds, felt cloth. Whatever it was in there, they wrapped it in something like a blanket, packed it up good, must have been valuable. I reached under the blanket, felt something hard and smooth, slowly lifted it up so I could get a look at it. I examined it a couple minutes, turned it around, let it gently back down again, didn't know if I should laugh or cry, thought I'd come a long way to be nowhere at all.

Going to work seemed stupid, I thought I had more important things to do. Lots of people think going to work is stupid but they go anyway, put bumper stickers on their cars that say, *I owe, I owe, so off to work I go*. I parked across from Alice, tried to think but fell asleep instead. About noon I woke up, thought the hell with Jerry, started the mini-truck. Our Joe wasn't dumb. He knew what we drove. He knew when we were watching. He watched us. I drove to a liquor store on Franklin for a coke, climbed back up the hill, this time taking the road on the other side of the canyon. I spotted Alice's house on the opposite ridge, back porch perched on forty-foot stilts anchored in the hillside. The twin O's in the big HOLLYWOOD sign stared down at the roof of her house like a pair of binoculars.

I found a shady spot to park the truck, stuffed the coke in my back pocket, slung the Nikon over my shoulder, followed the road on sneakers to the last house on the ridge. The asphalt ended at a gate and chain-link fence. Getting through was no problem. In a city of over three million people, you can usually count on somebody being there before you with a pair of wire snips. The hillside beyond the fence dropped steep through scrub brush and loose rock. I switched back and forth, worked my way down and then up the other side to the back of Alice's house. The planks in the side gate split apart just enough for me to get a ten-degree slice of the front yard and driveway. A red Porsche 911 was parked in the drive. I'd seen it before. Alice was home.

A wedge of fence shade gave me a sit-down spot out of the sun. My throat was thick with thirst. I popped the tab on the coke, forgot the can got all shook up coming down the hillside, it shot a geyser up the front of my shirt. The wedge of shade retreated to a thin line, disappeared into the fence. Another beautiful day in LA Not a cloud in the sky. Just a thin brown gruel, color of boiled beef. I watched drops of my sweat evaporate on the concrete. Heard the front door slam shut, a clip of heels on the walk. I put my eye to the gap between the boards, saw it was Alice. This is when things started to happen. The branches of the big oak tree in Alice's front yard trembled, and at first I thought it was just the wind but the air was dead calm. A body flew out of the oak. It was our Joe. Dressed in whites, clutching a tennis racket. Alice took one look and ran for the Porsche.

I got one shot over the top of the fence, put my shoulder to the gate, came out firing. Framed Alice as she struggled to key the door, with Joe background over her shoulder, tennis racket raised like a club.

Joe shouted, "Wait, Alice! We have to talk! It's important!"

Alice scrambled into the Porsche.

Joe reached out to her through the open door, called her name. In the viewfinder, his face was all pale and sweat-shiny. Alice slammed the door shut, locked it. Joe hammered on the window, shouted with each blow, "I love you! I love you! I love you!"

I swung the camera to Alice. She shielded her head with her arms, huddled over the steering wheel. Joe dropped the tennis racket onto the driveway, slowly lifted his polo shirt to his neck. A square patch of gauze covered the center of his chest. He fingered the tape securing the gauze to his skin, cried out, "Look, Alice! Look at me!"

Alice lifted her head from the steering wheel.

Joe's fingers jerked down, stripped the gauze from his chest. I released the shutter, zoomed the lens to 150 millimeter because I couldn't see what it was underneath the gauze. At first, I thought it was a tattoo, something silly, like the name *Alice* unfolding on a banner across a heart shape. But what he'd done wasn't silly at all.

What he'd done was dig a hole in his chest. The wound was a jagged eye a couple inches in diameter. Scabs ringed the outer edges, like he'd been digging at his flesh for weeks. Joe framed the wound with his thumb and forefinger, stretched the skin back, widened the hole to a gray and pink mass of bone. He stretched the hole wider still. Behind the bone, I saw something might have been his heart. His eyes swam back in his head. I thought he was going over, but he steadied. The wound ruptured, blood spurted down his belly, his body jerked. He gasped with each new spurt of blood. The way he gripped his chest, his gasping sounds, the blood spurting out, it was masturbation.

I shot until I ran out the roll. Then I called an ambulance.

When I walked in the door, Ben said, "What're you doing here, you're supposed to be at Alice's."

I tossed the roll of film on his desk, said, "Joe showed up."

Ben sat up, held the film between two cigar-sized fingers, said, "Come over here."

I came over. He wrapped his big arm around my neck, gave me a kiss on the cheek. I said, "Thanks, don't think I don't appreciate it, but I'd like a little money too," because they hadn't paid me since I started.

"We'd all like a little money," He said, which made me wonder about Ben and Jerry's cash flow situation. Ben set a cassette player on the corner of the desk, started recording, asked me a bunch of questions for what he said was the client report. It was hot in the room, the fan was going, it blew his hair up to little exclamation points every turn it made around the room. Ben wanted to know who was there, what happened, when it happened and where it happened. I told him everything I remembered, leaving out the part about me hiding behind the fence because I didn't want Jerry to get mad. Then I told Ben I had something down in the truck I wanted him to see.

He said, "Sure, bring it on up."

So I brought it up, a hundred-odd pounds one stair at a time, not sure Ben missed the point intentionally or really thought it was better I bring it up than he come down. I rolled the case into the office, set it on its side, eased the thing out of its nest and unwrapped the blanket. Ben didn't bother to get up, just peered at it over his desk.

I said, "So what is it?"

He cleared his throat, smiled, said, "You being a woman, you wouldn't know about these things, but what you've got here is a urinal. When you go into the men's room, they got several of these lined up for men to, you know."

"I know what men do when they go to the men's room." At least generally I did. "But the question I'm asking, is this just a urinal?"

Ben pushed himself out of his chair, walked around the desk, looked down at the thing, asked, "You have any reason to believe it's not a urinal?"

"My boyfriend, my ex-boyfriend I mean, he gave me this case to watch, said be careful, it's really valuable. Then he disappears, I haven't seen him for a week, so I open the case and this is what I find."

"Your boyfriend, he do a lot of drugs?"

"Sure, he does some," I said, just what I was thinking.

"Has a history of mental instability?"

I got down on my knees, lifted the top of the thing and shook it around, said, "No, you got the wrong idea, I was thinking there was something inside it."

Ben got down on the floor with me, took a pencil off his desk, tapped around the porcelain, listening for something neither of us knew what, said, "If this was a client situation . . ."

"This is not a client situation."

"Then get a hammer is the fastest way."

Somehow I didn't think I should be breaking the thing to pieces just yet. I said, "Maybe it's an antique, look at this here."

Ben turned the urinal around, looked near the base where I pointed. There was some handwriting there, said *R. Mutt 1917.*

He said, "I've seen people graffiti just about anything everywhere in bathrooms, but first time I've ever seen anybody write their name and visit date on a urinal."

I held the top of the crate up for Ben to see the lettering.

Ben said, "Greek, huh, what you've got here is a Greek toilet?"

"Russian."

"You already know what it is, what you ask me for?"

"I was hoping you might know what it said."

"I don't even know what language it is, you want me to tell you what it says?"

Like most men, Ben didn't like being shown wrong about anything. I said, "Ben, stop giving me so much shit, you know everything about this kind of business and I need some help here. How do I find out what it says?"

Ben looked shocked for a second, hearing me say he knew everything. He took the top of the crate, looked at it, said, "Second rule of detective work, you wanna know something, ask a librarian."

He pulled himself up by the corner of the desk, had none of that fat-man grace I'd always heard about, always moved slow and stumbling which is one reason I guess he rarely moved at all. He lowered himself into his chair, dialed a number from memory. Then his voice dropped a couple octaves and he started talking funny to whoever it was answered, called her *good-lookin'*, said he made about a hundred calls a day, but when he found himself dialing her number, a special little chill ran down his spine, asked if it was possible for souls to travel the phone lines, connect as blips of energy in the telephonic paradise of the AT&T switching network. He laughed at what she said back, sounded sexy doing it, said he had something written in Russian, could she help translate. Then he hung up, confided, "That was Rachel. Absolutely crazy about me. She's the closest thing to real sex I've got."

"How long you been seeing her?"

"Never actually seen her. Works at the main library downtown. Said she doesn't speak much Russian, but has a dictionary probably can help you figure it out."

I was confused about something, asked, "You like this woman?"

"Like does not begin to express. I asked Jerry to check her out once, he took a picture for me. She's about thirty-five, best age for a woman, seasoned but still young, you know? Wavy black hair, a nose that's a little too big, but still, it's got character. And her eyes, her eyes are liquid midnight, dark and full of Jewish soul."

"Why don't you go see her, ask her out?"

"Because she's crazy about me. I'm a Humphrey Bogart hardbody when I talk to her on the phone." Ben gestured at his body like an unwanted costume. "I show up to her in this, and the fat lady sings, and the game is over."

15

I came home late afternoon to rich scents of paint and canvas and male sweat, Billy b's smell, it settled like warm food in my belly. Didn't see Billy b around, everybody sounded gone. I leaned against the case, rested up a minute, thought about taking him inside me at the same time I could smell and feel him outside, was sorry he was gone, wished I could close my eyes and have him there, not saying anything, just inside and all around me.

I rolled the case into my room, parked it next to the first case, got ready to fall into bed, a long lonely sleep. A letter rested on the pillow below, LACE stamped in the upper left corner. I ripped open the envelope, read the letter inside, studied details of wording for any indication it was a joke. But the letter was straightforward, its meaning clear. My heart accelerated, the blood raced through my veins so fast I could feel the friction on my arterial walls. I had to move. I strode out of my room and into the kitchen, poured a glass of water from the tap, drank it down. I jumped straight into the air and was surprised that I landed on the kitchen floor, that I landed at all. I splashed water on my face, dried off, read the letter again. The words didn't change. I was in the show.

I went into Cass's studio, found her sleeping face down on the sheets, a book by Linda Seger just beyond her out-flung arm, something about screenwriting for Hollywood. I leaned over her, said, "Hey, wake up," but she didn't move. I went into Billy b's studio, handled his brushes, read the exotic colors of his paints. Cadmium. Vermilion. My head was light with joy. Everything I touched brought shivers of pleasure through my finger-tips. Dust floating in shafts of light sparkled brilliant like diamonds. The creak of my feet on the floorboards, the metal chime as I set down the coffee can of Billy b's brushes, sounded like music echoing down from the ceiling spaces. I stroked a sable-tipped brush with my forefinger, watched a dry fountain of dust plume from its edges. A light surrounded me, nothing I could see but there, crackling over my head.

Somebody like Billy b or Cass would take the news as the birthright of superior talent. Their sense of self and destiny was like granite. They stood firmly in their self-appointed spots, dared the world to move them. I was more like water, flowing this way and that in trying to understand who I was, what I wanted. Water can be a stream, a river, a lake, an ocean, a drop of rain. It can be held by rock, mud, glass, air, the slender stalk of a reed, the human body. Water is everywhere the same and everywhere different. Water is what shapes it. I'd always taken photographs, but it wasn't until that moment I thought of myself as a photographer.

The floor creaked with shifting weight. I didn't move, heard getting-up noises behind the screen of Billy b's sleeping corner. I was happy, more than happy, because I sometimes think happiness is nothing but empty-headed contentment, I was full of joy, it looked like Billy b was here, and I was going jump all over him, only it wasn't Billy b who staggered around the corner of the screen, it was a nude woman. She said, "I hafta pee. Where's the toilet?"

Nothing I could think of to say to that. No snappy retort or even simple directions. She looked like a rock-and-roll tramp. Black hair with purple highlights, heavy silver rings, a rhinestone nose stud, pendants, earrings and beads dangling from both ear-lobes. When I flicked a stunned forefinger in the direction of the bathroom, she turned and revealed a green and red dragon on her left shoulder blade, tail coiling down to meet her tail.

I thought, cool tattoo, bitch. Walked to the corner of the screen. The only way I wasn't going to kill somebody was if Billy b wasn't there. But he was, sitting up in bed, gazing out the window at the financial district skyline. I stood at the screen, stared at him.

It took him a while to notice me. He said, "Any coffee?"

"If there was, I'd throw you a cup. About ninety miles an hour."

"I warned you before, women liked to watch me paint."

"Just thought you had better taste."

"I don't know anything about taste. I'm into anti-taste."

"Makes me feel real special, that does."

"If you judge how I feel about you by my fidelity, you'll never get it. Most women come and go. I like you for other reasons than just sex."

"Because I'll make you famous."

Billy b said, "You got a registered letter from LACE."

His stare was amazing. No guilt at all. I wondered what forces of ego were required to forge a conscience such as his. Still, I couldn't get away from how compelling he was. Nothing more dangerous than a man who has lost the potential for self-doubt, whose certainty is so vital and magnetic that those of us who still question our place in the world are drawn into awed orbit.

He said, "Bobby told me you got in the show."

"How did Bobby know?"

"Bobby knows."

"Did Bobby pull strings?"

"What do you care how you got in?"

"He rigged it, is that what you're telling me?"

"I'm sorry you walked in when you did. I thought you worked afternoons. I didn't sleep with her to hurt you. I slept with her to get laid. We had no agreement to be monogamous. You knew I was the type to sleep around."

I said, "You want to sleep around, fine, just don't go thinking we got any special kind of romantic relationship. Now or later, when you talk to the press."

"What are you implying?"

"Nothing ever happened between us. You're a liar, a shallow fame seeker if you ever say it did."

That worried him. He said, "I know your look, your car, the details of your false I.D. If I want to hurt you, I'm in position to do it."

"You going to call the police?"

"You going to lie, say we weren't lovers?"

That's the worst thing about love relationships. Your partner always knows the weak spots. I said, "That was the wrong thing for me to say. I won't lie."

He pulled the sheet back, stood up, moved toward me, said, "Things are going well. You're in a major show. You have a new identity. You have to relax and let things happen. You have to trust a little bit."

Seeing him naked was the worst provocation. I didn't think about it. I planted my back foot and let it rip, a short right hook like I'd learned from my Pop. It caught Billy b flush on the jaw. I wanted to knock him down. A rush of satisfaction flushed through me. My knuckles tingled from the hit. I wanted to hit him again. Got ready to, pulled my fist back, stopped when I saw the look on his face. Shock. Fear. I knew the look from ever since I could remember, saw it a thousand times before on the face of my mom, my brothers, my sister, myself in the mirror, wondered if maybe the same thing in my pop wasn't in me sometimes, part of my blood, making me do things more like him than me.

When Cass found me at Gorky's, she was wearing shoes, designer jeans, silk shirt, black leather bag, the kind of sunglasses you buy for a hundred dollars, even wore lipstick, though she was careless putting it on, looked like a seven-year-old playing dress-up. Even when Cass tried to look normal she couldn't. She said, "I heard you and Billy b had a fight."

"I didn't have to hit him."

"He was happy you hit him."

"How so?"

"When I left, he was taking Polaroid pictures of his lip, said he wanted to do a painting of that exact moment."

I should have hit him twice, I should have broken his painting hand. Cass asked me if I wanted more coffee, maybe some dessert, she was buying. I should have been suspicious then, but I was distracted, didn't connect it with her sudden image change, thought she was just being nice. I said sure, cheesecake would be fine, watched her take the wallet from her big black bag, go up to the counter to order. I had to admire Billy b, always making art out of what happened to him, reminded me of this pillow my Mom had on her bed, bright yellow with needlepoint letters read, *When Life Gives You Lemons, Make Lemonade*. I looked at Cass's bag on the table, looked like a doctor's bag, sturdy leather with a brass clasp on top. I opened it up, saw Cass had her video camera inside with some other stuff. I set the camera aside, emptied the stuff out on the table, got a pen-knife from my camera bag and started cutting.

Cass got back with the coffee and cheesecake, shouted, "What are you doing, that bag cost over a hundred dollars!"

I finished cutting out the hole, about three inches up from the base, got some black tape from my camera bag, said, "You ever heard of a photographer named Walker Evans?"

"What does Walker Evans have to do with you cutting holes in my bag?"

"He used to have this trick, where he'd take pictures

of people on the New York subway without them knowing a picture was being taken."

I took Cass's video camera, set it in the bag so the lens looked out the small hole, wrapped the tape around so the camera stayed in one place. I had to catch Fleischer out. I knew my past and current lives were bound to meet at some time, the longer I prolonged that moment the greater the speed and force of the collision. It was that Einstein thing about $E=MC^2$, which I figured applied to personal problems as much as physics. I said, "I need you to get some things on tape for me."

Cass said, "You wreck my bag and now you want me to do you a favor?"

I led her to the phones in back, always try the obvious first, looked up Fleischer in the white pages, found a listing under Fleischer Security Services. I flipped over to the yellow pages. Fleischer had a quarter-page ad said he protected companies from burglary, embezzlement and terrorism.

I gave the company a call, asked for Mike Fleischer. Said to the secretary I was a friend of Victor Kabyenko, Fleischer would know the name. I waited on hold. Fleischer came on line, all he said was his name, waited for me to start explaining things. He wasn't going to say anything over the phone, he was going to let me do the talking. I said I was soliciting donations, told him another friend would drop by his office in about an hour to talk it over, hung up.

Cass asked, "Other friend? Who's this other friend?"

"You," I said.

We drove surface streets Hollywood to downtown. Fleischer Security Services occupied a suite of offices on a mid-level floor in a downtown bank high-rise. Nice-looking building, business must have been pretty good.

Cass said, "I'll do it if I get full dramatic rights."

"Rights to what?"

"Your life story."

"Are you crazy? What good will that do you?"

"I was talking to a friend of mine, a development executive at Paramount. We went to film school together. She thinks you're worth a small fortune."

"You told her about me?"

"Of course I didn't. I just mentioned a few hypotheticals."

"Like what if I knew that woman blew up the airport?"

"Sure, something like that. She's a smart woman. Knew it was you right away."

I stared at Cass, wanted to see if she was kidding. She wasn't. Seemed like every day somebody new was figuring how to make money off me. I took another look at the bag, decided even I couldn't tell where the lens was hidden if I looked at it from more than three feet away.

I said, "You have thirty minutes. If I don't see you in thirty minutes, I'm calling the police."

"Then we have a deal?"

I kicked her out the door, said, "What we have is to get moving."

On the videotape we made, this is what happens. Cass's new shoes jut in and out of frame as she walks down a long carpeted hallway. The carpet looks clean, new. The camera jostles, pans up to a door marked Fleischer Security Services. Cass's hand reaches in, turns the knob, pushes open the door. A receptionist glances up from behind a desk sandbagged across the entry, answers the phone, makes notes, hangs up, answers the phone again. Cass finally speaks up, says she's a friend of Victor Kabyenko, Mr Fleischer is expecting her. The receptionist looks doubtful but picks up the phone. She whispers something the microphone doesn't pick up, nods a couple of times, says in a surprised voice, "Mr Fleischer will see you now."

Fleischer himself is too busy writing something to

acknowledge Cass when she enters his office. He's a big man, football big, with a busted nose spread flat above his lips. His eyebrows are wormed with scars, the kind men get from taking a punch. My Pop's eyebrows look the same way. Pop used to say he'd take a shot above his eye, if it gave him an opening to the other guy's jaw. He would take one look at Fleischer, call him a bar-fighter and whore-fucker. Fleischer and my Pop would probably get along just fine.

Fleischer says, "I get all kinds of lunatics in my business. You might be surprised how many people think they can extort money out of my clients. I say you might be surprised, because I suspect you might be one of those lunatics." Fleischer smiles broadly at his punchline, shows offense was meant.

"I believe you knew a friend of mine," comes Cass's voice from behind the camera. Cass knows she's a lunatic, doesn't mind when accused of being one.

"Your friend?"

"Victor Kabyenko."

"Can't say that I do," Fleischer replies, doubtfully.

"But he knew you. Spoke fondly of you just moments before he died. That's why I'm here."

"Maybe he had me mixed up with somebody else."

"I don't think so, Mr Fleischer," Cass says, with just the right tone of assurance.

Fleischer's eyes drop from Cass's face, stare directly into the lens.

"Nice bag," he says.

"No it's not. It's a piece of shit."

"Mind if I took a look at it?"

"Sure I mind."

"You wouldn't happen to have a tape recorder in there, would you?"

The video image slants down to the carpet, shakes when the purse is opened. The camera is taped to the bottom of the bag, buried under a half-foot of books, cosmetics, snack foods, miscellaneous debris like you might find in a normal purse. The image tilts back up to Fleischer. He doesn't look completely convinced but doesn't look at the bag anymore, either.

Cass says, "My friend was supposed to deliver something to you."

"I don't know your friend, so I don't know what that might be," Fleischer smiles, playing along. He isn't going to give anything away to a couple of amateurs, he's going to listen, deny, act only when Cass leaves. But he knows, all right. The smile is a satisfied one.

"I guess I have the wrong Mr Fleischer."

The video image cranes up, swivels toward the door, then pans back to Fleischer, looking suddenly more anxious.

Cass says, "I'll be ready to make the delivery outside Johnny Rockets on Melrose at seven-thirty tomorrow evening. The price for delivery is ten thousand dollars, cash of course."

I walked around the block, flagged a taxi. I gave the driver twenty bucks, told him to wait outside the entrance of Fleischer's building, then returned to the mini-truck. I felt pretty nervous, because I figured these were serious killers, I'd feel awful guilty if something happened to Cass. No way Fleischer was going to let her go free and easy. I wouldn't, and I was an innocent babe compared to him. But I also figured he wouldn't try anything in his office. Five minutes before the deadline Cass hurried out of the building and hopped into the cab.

It didn't take long to spot Fleischer's man. I didn't recognize the guy behind the wheel, but the car was familiar. A Chevy Caprice. I slipped in behind, followed along. Traffic was heavy. The Caprice was keeping two cars behind the cab. It took three blocks to work my way around, signal and cut inside his front bumper. In that kind of traffic, a normal enough thing to do. The light ahead turned red. The cab stopped short. I could see Fleischer's guy in my rearview mirror, tapping his wheel. When the light switched to green, I didn't move. Horns sounded behind. I got out of the mini-truck, walked to the front, popped the hood. The Caprice rocked in reverse and rolled forward, but I had him pinned and it took him three or four tries to work out of it. By then, Cass and the cab were long gone.

Just in case Fleischer was working a double tail, Cass and I arranged a second dodge at a coffee house she knew in Hollywood. Cass paid the cab-driver, walked into the coffee house, bought a cappuccino, grabbed a table near the window, started reading a magazine. Left the magazine on the table, walked to the restrooms in back, snuck out the rear exit. I had the truck idling in the alley.

Cass said, "This development exec, she wants to take a meeting with you."

"I'm not the kind of person takes a meeting."

"She told me you made a living taking pictures of babies."

The past was what I wanted to get away from, I didn't want to talk about it, I said, "Since when did you go all Hollywood, talking to Paramount?"

"If I bring you in, I'll get first shot at the script, maybe a chance to direct."

"Lucky you."

"Really, Nina, you have to consider it a career move for yourself as well. It's what all the really interesting criminals are doing now. Television movies."

"You notice they got caught first."

"Even Charles Manson, he writes lyrics for Guns 'N' Roses."

"I thought you made documentaries, despised television."

"A chance like you comes around once a lifetime. If we can pull this deal off, neither of us will ever have to work another day of our lives."

I said, "I sure won't. I'll be in jail."

16

Next day, I'm standing in line at a 7–11 waiting to buy a coke, and okay I admit it, I've got an *Inquirer* mind, I see a copy at the counter rack, I pick it up, read it standing in line, might even buy a copy if the story really hooks me, and the story that morning really hooked me, the front headline went LOVE CRAZY FAN TEARS HEART OUT FOR TV ACTRESS. I grabbed a copy out of the rack, looked at it, saw the story was illustrated with photographs by some guy named Ben Harper, two shots of Joe terrorizing Alice with his tennis racket, one of him lifting his shirt up, the last one a close-up of the hole he'd dug in his chest. *Inquirer scoops world press, has photographer and reporter on scene*, the story read. Funny how I was standing right there the whole time, never even saw the guy. Like Jerry said, I didn't know anything, looked like I was blind too.

There was a big woman behind the reference desk at the main library when I went there, phone wedged between ear and shoulder while she leafed through the pages of a book. She wasn't Ben Steel big but big enough to appreciate the size of him, not be shocked by it. I waited until she finished helping the caller on the phone, felt kind of hopeful when I set the crate-top from the second case on the desk, said, "Ben Steel said I should come to you with this."

The woman said, "And what did Ben Steel say I should do with it?"

"Translate it, you see it's in Russian."

"I see that it's in CyrillIc. Technically, Cyrillic is an alphabet derived chiefly from the Greek and is used in the written form of Serbian, Bulgarian *and* Russian, among others."

I said, "Oh."

The phone rang again, she hurried off to answer it, looked like it was an important call because she turned her back on me to talk. A second librarian carried a long stack of books from behind the reference desk, the books came up to her eyebrows, she had a pencil between her teeth, she had to turn her head to the side to walk. She eased the stack onto the counter, saw the big woman was busy, asked, "May I help you?"

I said, "Well, Rachel was."

"I'm Rachel. Rosalie is busy just at the moment."

I said, "Oh."

Rachel saw the crate-top, the lettering stenciled on it.

When she looked at me I thought she was maybe blushing. She slipped the pencil out of her mouth, said, "You're from Ben Steel, aren't you?"

I asked, "You think you could help me translate this?"

She walked behind the stacks, came back with a big book she said was a Russian dictionary. She propped the crate-top on the counter, set the dictionary to the side, went to work. Rachel wasn't pretty but she had a face unlike any other, once you saw it you didn't forget. Her nose swept powerful as a mountain from the sharp ridge of her cheekbones, her thin-lipped mouth fell away in awe from the majesty of it. On another face such a nose would be tragic, but Rachel was blessed with a pair of eyes that were enormous and dark and Ben was right, they were soulful. I liked her hands too, long-fingered and delicate, she flipped through the pages of that dictionary as quick and precise as a piano player.

Rachel asked, "Where did you get this?"

I said, "It fell off a truck."

She saw I was kidding and wasn't, said, "I shouldn't have asked. I know the kind of work Ben does, but this is a little odd."

"Don't tell me, it says plumbing supplies."

"No. It says Hermitage Museum."

"What's that?"

"The biggest museum in Russia, one of the biggest in the world, in the West we still don't know how large.

Half of Central and Eastern Europe's art wound up in their collection after World War II."

"I don't suppose you have any idea why a urinal would be in a box from this Hermitage Museum, do you?"

"Perhaps as a joke?"

"Just what I was thinking."

"If I think of something, do you want me to call Ben?"

"Sure. You ever meet or see Ben?"

"Just on the phone."

I thought why not try, said, "He's a little different in person."

"How is he different?"

I thought about how big he was.

I said, "He's shy."

Rachel handed me the crate-top across the counter, said, "Unfortunately, so am I."

Cass and I got to Melrose Avenue a good couple hours early, climbed the fire escape of the building across the street, stood on the roof and looked around. Johnny Rockets is one of those Americana-type places selling '50s nostalgia to a generation born in the '60s and '70s. Hamburgers, fries, a jukebox, waitresses who chew gum, say, "Comin' right up, hon". Must be something to selling fatty foods like this, like it's all from the past, can't hurt you that way. Even a vegetarian could eat a hamburger here, think it's okay, I'm not eating this hamburger now, I'm eating it forty years ago.

We mounted the video camera on a tripod low to the ground, aimed it down at the street. Street traffic was constant, people walked up and down Melrose, shopping and hanging out, lots of witnesses in case Fleischer was tempted to try something violent. I imagined the way it would happen down there on the street, in front of the restaurant. I'd drive up, keep the motor running, stay calm, do the business.

Cass said, "You never told me what's in this case you're delivering."

I told her, I said, "A kitchen sink."

"I'm serious, you've involved me this far, you should tell me."

"I told you."

"Don't trust me then. What are you going to do with the ten thousand dollars, assuming they don't shoot you dead in the middle of the sidewalk?"

"There's a Holiday Inn a couple miles from here. I'm gonna rent a room, sleep for twelve hours."

"You're not coming back to the loft?"

I looked at her like, what are you getting at?

Cass said, "It's because of Billy b, right?"

I'd gone home the night before, shut myself in my room, could hear Billy b working late in his studio. Then he stopped working, knocked on my door, asked if I wanted a beer, if I wanted to talk. I said no to both, listened to him tell me how stubborn and unreasonable I was. Then he went back to work. Never did get much sleep.

I said, "I just want to sleep. No hassles. Just sleep."

At six-thirty, a tan Chevy Caprice cruised west, parked two blocks down. Five minutes later, a blue Chevy Caprice headed east, parked two blocks up. Maybe Fleischer got some kind of discount at the local Chevy dealership. I let them sit. A few minutes before seven-thirty, a guy got out of each car. Mid-thirties. Pot-bellied. Bad mustaches. Frick and Frack.

I pulled a copy of that day's *Los Angeles Times* from my back pocket, set it on the roof in front of the camera, said, "Remember, no cuts. Get a shot of the date on the newspaper, pan up, film what you see happening. Don't forget close-ups so these guys can be identified."

Cass put her eye to the viewfinder, zoomed the lens in and out, said, 'I'll use a trick we learned in film school called the choker."

I handed over the letters from Kabyenko to Fleischer. "When it's over, take the tape, make a copy. Put the tape in a large envelope. Put these letters in with it. Seal the envelope, address it to Sergeant Martinez, from Madame Zero. Take the envelope down to the police station on

Wilshire, give it to the man personally, then get out before he opens it."

"I'll see you again, right? You're not planning to disappear?"

"Not unless something goes wrong," I said.

I climbed down the fire escape. The mini-truck was in the back parking lot. I sat for a moment behind the wheel, thought about it, took a few deep breaths, saw how much my hands shook. I started the engine, floored it. The truck came roaring out of the back alley spitting gravel, cut across a lane of traffic, squealed to a stop in the red zone at the corner of Johnny Rockets. I left the driver's side door winged-open, the motor running, got to the back bed in four swift strides.

Frick and Frack came up to me from opposite directions. Up close, they didn't look so identical. Same round face, dead brown eyes, but Frick was a couple years older. Had a few more lines than Frack, a couple gray hairs. He was the one carrying the money, the one who started talking to me right away, calling me girl, saying I'd changed so much he hardly recognized me, he was the one they wanted me to watch while Frack stopped at the passenger door, tried to open it. When he couldn't, he reversed his path, skirted the hood to get to the driver's side.

I said to Frick, "I got a friend on the roof with a scope-sight dead center on your chest." I pointed to a rooftop far away from Cass. "He sees anything go wrong, I don't get out clean in three minutes, he pierces your lung, you understand me?"

Frick said, "You got no friend on the roof."

"Don't take me for an idiot, you'll live longer."

Frick smiled, backed down. He called out, "Hey, Frack."

His brother backed away from the driver's side, joined us on the sidewalk. I dropped the gate, let them see the case. Frick opened the brown paper bag, counted five bundles of twenties. He said, "I showed you mine, you show me yours."

I grabbed one end of the case, told him to grab the other. We hoisted the case off the back bed, set it down on the sidewalk. Frack grabbed at the lock, tried to open it. I pulled the key out of my side pocket, held it up, said, "The money."

Frack said, "What are you going to do with all that cash?"

"Buy a bottle, drive to Mexico."

"For a sweet young thing, you got this worked out pretty good."

Frick said, "Key and bag change hands same time."

I held out the key. Our fingers met in the middle. He tossed the sack. I let go. Frick knelt at the case, keyed the lock, opened it. Summer in LA, seven-thirty at night, it's half-dark out, I figured Kabyenko's trick would still work, they wouldn't know one from another. Frick saw the crating, the Russian lettering, said, "Looks good."

I said, "Kabyenko left a note. Said some stuff about this Fleischer guy."

Frack said, "Let's see it."

I moved toward the open driver's door, slipped into the seat, jumped on the gas. The truck screamed from the curb, missed giving a guy in a BMW emergency heart surgery by half an inch. I jerked the wheel back, took one look out my rearview mirror. Frick and Frack stood over the case, watched me drive off. Nothing they could do about it, still had no idea what happened, what they didn't have beneath the crating. I hung a suicide left across traffic, looked for anybody trying to follow. The rearview was clear. I laughed, thought, what idiots.

The woman behind the desk at the Holiday Inn looked at me like I was some kind of criminal when I walked up with my paper bag and asked for a second-floor single off the street. I was afraid she recognised me, but it was just the brown paper bag, the black hair and pierced nose, guess I didn't look like her normal guest. She asked, "Will that be cash?"

I knelt over the brown paper bag, opened it, peeled off five twenties from the top of the first stack.

"Comes to eighty-eight ninety-five," the clerk said.

The first twenty I laid out on the desk was good. The other four weren't twenties at all, they were sheets of paper, some size and color as cash. I knelt over the sack again, tore open another bundle. One twenty on top, nothing but paper beneath. Same result with the rest. Fleischer probably used the same trick with the money in the exploding briefcase. Kabyenko and these guys thought alike, deserved each other. I counted the five good twenties out to the clerk, got eleven dollars, five cents in change from my ten thousand.

The dream I had that night, two guys were chasing me. Looked a little like Frick and Frack, except they were dressed in whites, carried tennis rackets. They were trying to hit me over the head, shouting they loved me. I jumped, high as I could, started to fly, great feeling, looked down. Frick and Frack had shotguns, started shooting at me.

Banging on the door woke me sometime after midnight. I staggered out of bed, stuffed myself into my pants one leg at a time, hopped to the sliding glass door, didn't know who it was at the front door, wanted to check my escape route. This was the time I started wishing I carried a gun, in case it was somebody I didn't want to talk to. The banging didn't stop. I went over to the door, eyed the peep hole. It was Cass. I unlocked everything, let her in.

Cass turned on the light, asked, "Are you sleeping?"

I went back to the bed and fell on it.

Someone else said, "Maybe we should come back tomorrow."

I opened my eyes, sat up. A woman stood next to Cass. About thirty years old. Wore a silk blouse, mini-skirt, tights and ostrich-skin cowboy boots, the kind that cost eight hundred bucks a pair. Hair pulled back in a pony-tail. Very deft touch with the make-up. Light eye-shadow, lipstick a watery red. Feminine but tough.

The woman said, "You must be Nina. Or do you still prefer Mary?"

I said to Cass, "This is a joke?"

A business card materialized between the woman's thumb and forefinger, she said, "Donna Wanker, Paramount Television. Vice President, Development." Said it that way too, each word capitalilzed.

Cass put her arm around Donna, who smiled with so many teeth showing I thought she was gonna bite me. Cass said, "This is the woman I was telling you about, the one I went to film school with."

Donna said, "We're talking MOW, major network, top stars. With this kind of package, we think we can get Madonna."

"Get her to do what?"

"To play you, of course. Movie-Of-the-Week. A star

199

of Madonna's caliber won't do just any story. And television? Forget it. But this, she can't pass up. A perfect girl-next-door-turned-most-wanted story."

I said, "Uh-huh."

Donna said, "Cass, she sounds less than enthusiastic. I thought you talked to her."

"I did, Donna. I think she's sitting on the fence now, listening to offers."

Donna sat on the edge of the bed, tried to hook my eyes with a look warm and trustworthy the same time it was mercenary. She said, "You haven't talked to anybody else, have you?"

I looked at Cass, said, "You could have waited. Just another couple days."

Donna said, "Too late. The strategy now is to lock the rights up early."

I said, "Lock them up."

Donna said, "Lock them up tight before relatives of the victims can file suit and garnish earnings."

I wasn't crazy to have anything of mine locked up, I wanted to point out I was the victim in this situation, but the woman started to talk, wouldn't stop. She said, "You should listen to me, I know my job. We've worked with some of the top criminals in the business. Love-triangle killers, mass murderers, assassins. We always pay going rates for true-crime stories. Can't have a homicidal maniac unhappy about his contract, if you get what I mean. It's to your benefit to sign a contract now. For example, have you ever thought about how you're going to pay your legal expenses?"

"But I haven't been arrested yet."

Cass said, "Beside the point. You will be."

Donna said, "And please forgive me for speaking a hard truth here, but what if you're killed in a shoot-out with the police? Wouldn't you feel better knowing your mother would be taken care of, not to mention her pride in seeing a top star like Madonna play the lead role in a movie about her daughter's life?"

I said, "How about you two get out of here."

"But if you get killed without a signed contract, your family won't get a dime!"

I got up, opened the door.

Cass said, "Do you want that tape delivered to Sergeant Martinez or not?"

"You still have it?"

"You told me to get it copied first. Takes time."

Donna was a real problem-solver, she said, "The studio has state of the art video facilities. No problem to copy it there, any time day or night."

I shut the door, said to Cass, "I can't believe you're blackmailing me."

"I can't understand why I'm doing all these favors for you, practically put my life at risk for you this afternoon, bring you this great deal tonight, great for you, great for everybody, and you just throw me out. I think to myself, why should I continue to do favors for somebody so ungrateful? Do you know what I mean?"

Donna said, "The contract is in my purse, ready to sign, fifty thousand for the rights, standard option agreement, of course."

I signed first, asked later, "What do you mean, standard option agreement?"

Cass explained, "It means you get ten per cent of the fifty thousand up front, the rest when they actually make the picture."

"And if they don't make the picture?"

"You don't get the money."

I said to Cass, "What do you get, they let you write the script?"

Donna said, "New writer, TV project, about forty thousand."

"One of those options again?"

"No, she gets it all."

"So my story, she gets four times more than me?"

"That's right."

"Lucky her," I said.

17

Jerry was sitting at Ben's desk cleaning a handgun when I stopped in the office. Had the cylinder flipped open, stared at me through the empty bullet chambers, pretended to look for dirt or powder or whatever it is you look for when you clean a gun.

I said, "You must be Ben Harper."

He looked at me kind of funny, said, "What's the matter, you forget my name already?"

"Didn't forget at all, never knew. Maybe Ben's Ben Harper, you're Jerry Steel, you do the *Star* while Ben does the *Inquirer*."

"You saw the article."

"Sure did."

"Like I said, you don't know anything."

I got a little steamed at that because the reason I didn't know anything was because nobody would tell me, so I said, "What is this, you go around advertising yourself as this hotshot detective but you're really a trash journalist, a lying one too."

Jerry got this gleam in his eye, like he was happy I got mad at him, was the kind of guy didn't mind a woman with a little fight in her. He said, "Pays the rent, helps me do what I really like doing."

"What's that?"

"Look for missing persons."

That didn't make me feel too secure, I wondered what he would do if he knew who I really was, I said, "Oh."

"Besides, you're the one going around breaking into houses, looking for drugs in toilets, importing God-knows-what all the way from Russia. Seems to me you might be doing a little lying too."

I shut up for a while. Jerry wound a small piece of cloth around a metal rod, soaked the cloth in solvent, ran it through the chambers, one by one. The bullets were lined up like pawns along the edge of the desk. He asked, "You ever shoot a gun?"

"An old .22 rifle a couple times, with my Pop. Never a pistol."

"You want to learn?"

I inched closer to the desk and looked at the thing in his hand. The grip was dark walnut, the cylinder and barrel flat blue steel. Mechanically, it was elegant, with a seductive precision in the spin and click of the cylinder, the cock and snap of the hammer. I knew the gun was evil, an extension of the male desire to kill something just by willing it to happen.

I told Jerry hell yes, I wanted to learn.

Jerry drove out to the desert to shoot, because even though you can go to a gun club and shoot legally in the city, he hated paying money to shoot his guns. When you grow up someplace where you walk out your back door to shoot, it grates you to have to pay for it. We got take-out at an Italian deli in Hollywood, made a picnic out of it. About twenty miles past Mojave, Jerry took a cross-road that stretched flat across the desert floor toward the Tehachapi Mountains to the north. The heat shimmered off the sand like it was so hot even the air couldn't take it, had to jump away. A dozen miles from the freeway, a dirt road forked off through the scrub brush and dust. The hills didn't look that far away, but the road was badly rutted all the way through, washed damn near out in places.

I shouted out over the thump of potholes and slinging gravel, "Hey, Jerry, you ever hear of a guy called Mike Fleischer?"

He glanced at me like he'd just heard the shake of a rattlesnake's tail.

"What kinda scam are you working on, anyway?"

"No scam. Just heard about him."

"Fleischer is the best in the business. Also the most dangerous. Learned some nasty shit working as an agent in Berlin."

"You mean, like CIA?"

"Retired. You ever run across him, you should smile, shake his hand real polite, and sneak away fast as you can."

"What if you can't?"

"I know two guys once did a little business with Fleischer. One of them lived long enough to make some good money at it."

"What about the other guy?"

"The other guy, he did something Fleischer didn't like, then tried to run to Mexico. Fleischer had him sent back. One body part at a time. In little packages mailed to the guy's wife, mother, best friend. The guy was still alive by package number twelve. The thirteenth package was his head."

I didn't ask Jerry any more questions about Fleischer.

The road dead-ended in a canyon carved out by flash floods. A couple cottonwoods scraped out a living against the canyon wall. The shade was cool as heaven. Jerry sat me down under the cottonwoods, explained some rules to keep in my head when around a gun. The first rule is you can kill somebody without intending so you damn well better be careful. He spun the cylinder, cocked the hammer, worked the safety, ran his fingers along the barrel while he talked. He asked if I was ready to hold it. I said sure. The walnut grip was warm from his hand. I did all the things Jerry told me to do. Checked the safety first, dropped the cylinder to see if it was loaded. Then I just held it, looked at its smoothly machined surfaces, got to know it by touch.

The long shape of the barrel, the way the bullets are stored in the round cylinder, the act of shooting something out of a barrel, it all seemed foreign to my anatomy and consciousness. Watching Jerry, the way he'd carry the gun with loose confidence at his side, the easy familiarity when he touched it, was like watching a guy and his penis. I heard of this detective in New York City could tell when a guy was carrying a concealed weapon by what he called the touch factor. The guy always reached to touch the gun where it was hidden, to reassure himself. Considering how often men use this same gesture with their penis, I wondered if men are afraid their penis is going to disappear, have to touch it all the time to reassure themselves it's still there.

Jerry told me it was important to shoot someplace where the bullet wouldn't carry so far you couldn't see it stop. Shooting in the open desert, you could accidentally kill a guy you didn't see walking half a mile away. We dropped down into the dry river bed and climbed upstream for a quarter mile before we found the perfect spot, a washed-down log wedged against a switch-back. Jetty set an empty beer can on the log. He paced off ten yards, drew a line in the dirt with the toe of his Tony Lama.

"This is the way you don't shoot."

He turned profile to the beer can, drew his breath, sighted down the long skin of his up-raised arm, and my God, the noise of that thing going off knocked me back two feet. The beer can skittered off the log.

"Winged it," he said.

I picked up the can. There was a jagged cut a quarter inch from the top. I set the can on the log, walked back behind the line. Jerry said the way he shot wasn't by the book, but it was more interesting to him, like the way they dueled in the old days. While he was talking to me, real casual like, he turned his head, raised his arm, fired. This time he took out the center of the can.

He set up a new can, said, "Your turn."

Just holding the gun scared me some, but I wasn't going to let myself be scared, even question if it was the right thing to do. I'd let the doubts come later. I did what Jerry said. Faced the target, bent my knees, cupped right hand in left, rested chin against shoulder for a steady sight.

Jerry said, "Breathe softly in, hold your breath, and squeeze the trigger before you count to four."

My nerves were anything but steady, and even though I followed his instructions, that beer can buzzed around the sight like a fly. It didn't stop moving by the time I counted four, Jerry didn't say what to do if that happened, so I jerked the trigger. A violent shock went rippling through my body. It was like the pistol was alive for an instant, tried to jump out of my hands. The hellish noise of the thing going off scared me blank.

"Still a virgin," he said.

I looked at him, like, what are you talking about?

Jerry read the look, explained, "Not you, the can."

I laughed, because there it was again, the male sex thing. I imagined myself holding a penis, almost dropped the gun in the dirt.

Jerry came up behind, said, "You gotta relax a little."

I felt his hands on my shoulders, working the muscles below the neck. His hands on my body felt good. When he backed off, I lowered the sight onto the target, fired, missed again.

"This distance, you gotta be a good shot to hit somethin' so little as a beer can. What say we move up a bit?"

Jerry walked to the log, took five long strides away, drew another line in the dirt with the toe of his boot. He said, "Now just shoot."

I emptied out the gun. Zero for six.

Jerry said, "Bound to hit it sooner or later. Pure chance if nothing else."

I hit the can on my eleventh try, a couple more times shooting to eighteen. Jerry showed off after that, set up six beer cans and tried to pop them off one by one. I got out my camera, looked at Jerry new ways I hadn't seen before. He was good at shooting, even just playing around, serious and cocky at the same time. He looked pretty sexy too, particularly when I asked him to take off his shirt. I circled to where the setting sun lit up his skin, the desert stretched flat below him. He crossed his arms over his naked chest, pistol cocked by his cheek, grinned. That was the picture I was waiting to happen. That was Jerry, boy-sexy and dangerous.

It was getting dark when we finished shooting out the box. My hand hurt like hell. Jerry said it was because percussion shocks the joints, promised a little bit of Old Kentucky bourbon would take the edge off the pain. We walked to the van, knocked back a few slugs of OK, found ourselves a rock to sit on and went to work making the take-out disappear. We didn't talk much. Just ate. When we'd eaten all we could and still hold it down, we settled back against the rock, watched the stars come out. It was a comfortable feeling, sitting out in the country under the stars with a boy, like when I was seventeen and went to the canyons with the gang and paired off with the guy I was going out with at the time. The talk was familiar and easy, the usual things people from small town backgrounds talk about when just getting to know each other, like your best friends and what your family is like, little things about your home town that you missed or you hated.

Jerry asked, "Ever gonna go back, you know, like live there again?"

"Hate it, hate small towns, no way I'll ever live in one again," I said. I didn't want to go back. Ever. But then I'd hear or see or smell something that reminded me of it, not of the town specifically, but of the people who lived there and the kind of lives they lived, and I'd feel this ache inside that made me smile at the same time it hurt.

"What about you? You ever going back?"

"I have this fantasy, someday I'll build a big split-level cabin on the lake, up in Tahoe. I'll own a convertible Corvette, drive down to Stockton every now and then to tool around the streets, see a friend, maybe just gas up where everybody can see me, see I made it big after all."

Jerry rolled off the rock, went back to the van to get the bourbon. He gave me the first slug. I took it, handed back the bottle. He put the bottle to his lips, looked angry about something. He said, "Stupid small-town rural redneck asshole kind of fantasy, if you ask me."

I said, "I don't know, doesn't sound so bad."

"More likely I'll end up dead in an alley someplace, shot in the back by somebody never saw my face."

"You think you're gonna die young?"

I was curious to hear his answer because I was thinking about this question myself. I never used to worry about it, when I had a job, an apartment, a predictable life. But lately I was feeling like that rabbit strayed far from the burrow, didn't even know where the burrow was anymore. The rabbits who remain a five-second sprint from the safety of the ground, those are the ones live long lives.

Jerry said, "Never thought I'd see twenty-one. But now that I've reached the ripe old age of twenty-eight, well, thirty looks damn near possible. But forty? Forty is when they start fitting you for a cane. Forty is old. May as well be dead if I don't have what I want by then."

We drank some more, I started to get a buzz going and leaned back to watch the stars, and then there was Jerry's face in front of me, and it was his sexy full mouth I was watching and he was kissing me. I didn't stop him. The thing with Billy b left me feeling empty inside and I needed to fill it up with something and Jerry was just the something I needed. We kissed some time under the stars, then had half-drunk, half-clothed sex in the back of the van. Small-town sex. I liked that, having sex in the back of a van in the desert night with a boy who reminded me of the small-town bad boys I knew back home when I first discovered sex. I needed to want somebody, I needed somebody to think I was sexy, somebody I thought I knew, I thought I could control. Anything was better than emptiness, and in moonlight Jerry looked a lot better than just anything.

I drove back to the loft in the blue hour, the hour before dawn when the sky turns from black to liquid blue, the streets and buildings look fantastic in that light, like an aquarium city. While I was driving, it was like this melody played inside me, a sweet song that makes me smile same time I know it has a sad ending, this is how I feel most times I meet a new boy. I liked Jerry but not so much it was going to change my life. Coming back from the desert I'd thought about what I should say to him, and when we got to Hollywood finally I just said it. I had a real nice time, but we maybe shouldn't count on the thing between us being too regular. It wasn't that I didn't like him enough, it was just that my life was kind of hectic, and seeing as I couldn't tell which way events were going to turn out, we couldn't expect this to be too steady a thing. Jerry said, "You talk like you think I want to get serious, marry you." Then he pulled me down on top of him and we did it a second time, parked on the street, longer and slower.

Coming up San Pedro three cop cars sped into my rearview mirror emergency lights flashing, scared the shit out of me, I jerked the truck to the side of the road thinking it happened so fast I didn't have a chance, but the cop cars sped past, not at all interested in me. I pulled back onto the road, turned toward the street the loft was on, saw police cars blocked the street both directions. Roof lights flashed red and blue. A helicopter clattered overhead. Three men in flak jackets stood on the roof of the building across from the loft. One watched the circling helicopter. The others had rifles pointed down at the windows.

I missed the turn, drove a couple miles gripped by a bad case of the shakes. Got so scared I couldn't think. Saw two more cop cars come barreling down the road, then an ambulance. The ambulance, that worried me, thinking something must have happened to Billy b, to Cass. I turned on the radio, scanned the news channels, didn't hear anything about what I saw happening. I pulled the truck around, drove back.

A small crowd stood behind the police line, mostly homeless, a few early morning workers stopped to gawk. The police milled around like it was all over except the coffee. The ambulance driver was drinking a cup with the cops, laughing about something. One of the cops had a bandage around his finger, looked like he'd cut himself. Another cop was limping around, like he was trying to walk off a charley-horse. On the other side of the intersection, a raggedy old man pushed a shopping cart loaded with bottles and cans. I jaywalked across to give him a dollar, ask a few questions.

He saw it all, he said, he was working that very street looking for raw materials, that was his business, called himself a raw materials trader, when a whole mess of police cars come barreling around the corner, led by one huge armored-looking vehicle. There was a film crew on the street filming the whole thing, thought it was a movie at first, then he saw this pretty newscaster he knew, saw it was just TV. The armored car, it squeals to a stop in the middle of the street, the doors spring open, and a dozen men come running out, all wearing flak jackets and baseball caps, carrying real big guns. Meanwhile, the police cars slide cross-wise on the street, so nobody can make a getaway on wheels. The cops they draw their littler guns and point the business ends over the hoods of their cars. The guys in baseball caps are what they call a SWAT team, which he said was short for Soldiers that Whacks Assassins and Terrorists. And team is what they were. It all unfolded like a football play, with guys rushing here and there according to a plan looked like confusion to somebody who didn't know better. They all run into this one building, some from the front, the rest from the back. He thought for sure there was going to be blood and gore because all of a sudden

217

three big bangs went off and he heard a bunch of shouting coming from inside the building. But that was pretty much all that happened. No smoke or fire or bodies falling out of windows or nothing. It was pretty to watch, though, he had to admit, even if the ending came a little short of expectation.

I gave him another dollar, said it was just like seeing the thing happen myself. Drove around for a while, finally headed up to the observatory at Griffith Park. I watched the city stir beneath its brown blanket of smog, the sunlight glint off the downtown high-rises and evaporate in the thick marine air to the west. Damn Billy b, it had to be him told the police about me. Probably in jail now, a pack of hungry reporters howling outside, ready to slash his name across the morning papers. Could have been Cass, too. I signed the contract with Wanker night before last. If I disappear, it means no headlines, no trial, no ending, no story. I get killed in a police shoot out it's gotta be good for ratings. The only way I'd learn exactly who it was betrayed me would be pointing a gun at somebody's head, asking direct.

When I walked through the door of Steel Investigations, Ben wouldn't look at me, he wore a floppy Gold Gym sweatshirt, held in his fist a quart-sized bottle of something orange, looked like carrot juice. People were changing all around me in those days, sometimes I felt like a brass ring people were grabbing at, but I never expected Ben to change because I'd never seen somebody seemed so stuck in bad habits before. I looked around the office, didn't see any pizza boxes, saw instead a plastic bucket of lettuce on his desk.

I said, "Ben, what's the matter, you sick or something?"

He reached into his desk drawer, counted out three hundred and fifty dollars, said, "Things used to be quiet around here, nothing to do but sit around, answer the phone, eat what I want, turn a quick buck or two on jobs for the *Inquirer*. Ever since you joined up all kinds of weird things started happening."

I swept the cash into my pocket, said, "What you talking about?"

"Mike Fleischer is what I'm talking about. You know him?"

"I heard of him."

"I got a call this morning, talked to him once or twice before, the guy always gets the hairs on the back of my head to stand on end. He said he was looking for somebody wheeling a big black case around, the way he described that somebody sounded a hell of a lot like you."

"What did you tell him?"

"Said I'd never seen you, but he has reason to think

different. You remember when you first came here, you said you were sent by somebody, Pat Nolan it was? Nolan told Fleischer he met somebody looked like you, said he sent her to me."

Frick and Frack, they knew what I looked like since the day before yesterday, this Fleischer guy was calling everybody he knew, asking if they'd seen me. I didn't know if I should tell Ben everything or nothing, decided I'd tell him nothing, not because I didn't trust him, because I wanted to keep him out of trouble if I could. I said, "Don't worry about Fleischer, I can handle him."

Ben got red in the face, just about shouted, "You can't handle a guy like Fleischer. He wants something, don't fuck around, give it to him. I knew somebody once tried to cheat Fleischer, he was sent home in boxes, one box at a time, one body part per box, kept alive until the thirteenth box was sent, the thirteenth box was his head."

I said, "Okay, I get it, the guy's dangerous."

Ben took out his pack of Luckies, fumbled one out of the pack, lit it with his silver Zippo, said, "One other thing. Rachel called."

I put it together, the sweatshirt, the carrot juice, the lettuce. I walked up behind him, felt his muscles, tried to lift him out of his chair, said, "Feels like you lost some weight."

"Five pounds already, only seventy more before I'm down to two-twenty."

220

"You ask her out?"

"She asked me. Said she understood what it was to be shy, said she was shy herself, thought it was time to have a little courage, give something a chance."

"When you going out?"

"Next week. I'm scared shitless. I haven't been on a date in . . ." Ben tilted his head back, tried to remember, asked, "Do prostitutes count?"

I walked over to Hollywood Boulevard to use the pay phones, called the loft. The answering machine picked up on the third ring. I listened to Billy b's taped voice, didn't want to leave a message with the law on the other end, hung up saying nothing. I called LA County Jail next, said I was a friend of Billy b and Cass Mitchel, heard they'd been arrested, I needed to post their bail. The clerk looked it up, said they didn't have any record of persons under that name.

I dialed another number, waited to hear a voice.

The voice said, "Hello?"

I said, "Hi, it's me."

"Baby, where are you?"

"I'm in hell, Mom."

"Are you okay?"

"Just fine."

"We've all been worried sick."

"Me too. Gotta go."

"Are you eating enough?"

"They're tracing the call, Mom."

"Wait, don't go yet."

"Love you lots."

I hung up, walked around Hollywood until dark, couldn't think of anything to do except eat what I wanted, look at things I had no reason to buy. I'd lived by my wits the past two weeks, seemed I was about to die by them. Fleischer knew what I looked like, was hunting me all over the city, I didn't want to be around when he found me. The cops had to know what I looked like too, Billy b didn't have to say a thing with Bobby Easter doing publicity. Staying on the run didn't make much sense anymore. I was sure the cops had the case. Without the case, I had nothing to bargain with, no way to prove it was all a mistake. Could have been me the guilty one as easy as Wrex, Frick and Frack, anybody.

I stopped in a liquor store. Worrying about things wasn't going to help much. I bought a pint of Jack Daniels, thought about doing two of my favorite things, then turning myself in next morning. Like that woman at the phone booth said, you can't fuck your boyfriend in jail, figured I'd go find the closest thing to a boyfriend I had going.

And there was Jerry, handsome as hell, had his boots up on Ben's desk when I got in, listening to a cassette tape of Elvis Presley on the boom-box. He grinned seeing me come in, like I just improved the day he was having a hundred per cent. "Heartbreak Hotel" was what Elvis was singing. Jerry jumped up from his chair, sang along and wiggled his hips and swept the hair out of his eyes just like Elvis used to do. Just about every woman I met growing up thought Elvis was the perfect man. Sensitive, brooding, talented, handsome as a god. My mom's friends, half of them had pictures of Jesus Christ and Elvis Presley side by side in the living room. So many women have dreamed of making love to Elvis if this wasn't a good Protestant country Elvis would have ascended to formal divinity when he died, be worshipped to this day as a fertility god. At the dead center of his divinity is a sexuality so intense it makes women give up their hearts and last bit of good sense. Seeing Jerry do Elvis made me want to jump all over him.

I stripped the seal from the Jack Daniels, slugged down a shot, corked the bottle, tossed it to Jerry when the song ended. He nipped at it, not his usual chug-a-lug, locked the pint in the top right desk drawer. Sex or no sex, the one thing I intended to do that night was drink.

I said, "Where you putting that bottle?"

"I need you sober tonight," he said, and I resented the way he said it, like maybe I had a drinking problem, which maybe was true and maybe was not, but he wasn't the one to point it out to me, not beer-a-minute Jerry.

"Since when you tell me when I can or can't drink?"

He opened the desk drawer, tossed the bottle back, said, "Drink away, I don't care. But I have this job to do tonight and I said to myself you were just the person to help me."

I uncapped the bottle, took a taste just to make my point, asked, "What is it you want me to do?"

"Drive," he said, and the way he said it was real provocative, like he was talking about sex. He knew I was proud of my driving, couldn't resist an opportunity to show off to him.

"You're not going to do anything illegal? No way in hell am I going to get involved in drugs or stealing or explosives or anything like that and if you tell me one thing but it turns out you lied to me I swear to God, Jerry, I'll cook your balls in a microwave."

He told me to relax, said there was nothing illegal to it at all. He had a car repossession to do. Needed somebody to watch his back, drive the van in case he had to get out of there fast or follow behind if he made the repo clean.

"I don't know, some poor stiff gets laid off his job, can't make his payments, I'm the last one to come take his truck."

Jerry was insulted, said, "I'm not going to repo anything from a working man, no money in it anyway. Some yuppie buys more Beamer he can afford, some Hollywood hotshot gets a top-of-the-line Porsche to impress the babes, they're just stealing from the system, and if you let them get away with it now, they'll keep stealing until you get something like the Savings-and-Loan crisis. But a blue-collar repo, that I'd never do."

I said, "Give me the keys, let's roll."

I wanted Jerry to come over and kiss me, but he didn't, he turned like he was going straight for the door, so I warned him I was coming with a whoop, jumped up on his back and bit his ear. He grabbed my legs so I fit piggyback style, asked me what I was doing. I said he was my horse, I was going to ride him into the ground, said this while I was kissing and biting his neck. He asked me if I knew what horses did to get rid of their riders. I said go ahead and try, thinking he might buck a little. Instead, he stumbled backward, slammed me against the wall. I thought he was right, that was what a smart horse might do, try to wipe you out against a tree. My legs lost their grip and Jerry spun around and we were face to face. His eyes went dark and it was like the darkness was his passion and it was pouring out all around me. I asked him what he was going to do now. Only it wasn't a polite question. It was a taunt.

His answer was to lift me off my feet. I wrapped my

legs around him again, from the front this time. He walked me over to the desk, cleared it with a sweep of his arm. He dropped me on the surface and I pulled him down after, ripped at his shirt, his belt, his pants, at anything in the way of the rush of skin on skin. It was violent, the way we thrust against each other, it was power we were testing, who was the strongest, would end up controlling the other.

Jerry drove the van over the hill from Hollywood, out to Encino. He said we were going to repo a new Mercedes 500 SL convertible parked in the underground garage of a Ventura Boulevard condo complex. No guard, the problem was getting around the remote control gates. Once he got in the car, he'd find the beeper so he could get out again.

I said, "I thought your thing was missing persons."

He answered it was a lot easier finding cars, people could hide almost anywhere, be almost anybody. He said, "A cute little runaway thirteen years old, after a year on the streets doing drugs and hooking, what with the change of hairstyle and color and make-up and hard life, her own parents wouldn't even know her."

His smile at me was funny. I wondered if he knew, was playing along like he didn't, waiting. Stupid of me to ask the question in the first place, like a dare. I was sure he didn't know. Later that night, after making love again, I'd tell him. Wouldn't be cute about it, wouldn't make him guess. Just say it flat out.

Jerry pulled off the freeway at Ventura Boulevard, the street was all storefronts and ad signs, another Southern California town where the entire culture revolves around going out and buying stuff. He turned left off Ventura, half a block up the hill he cut the engine, coasted to the curb. Across the street was the condo complex, I could see the drive curving down behind locked gates to an underground parking garage.

Jerry said, "If something goes wrong, don't be a hero. Play dumb. If I come out running, be ready to motor in a hurry."

A car door slammed, had that underground echo sound. The gates across the way rolled open, a convertible Mustang roared onto the street. Jerry skirted the edge of the drive, slipped inside the gate as it rolled shut, the dark of his black jeans jacket disappeared behind the first parked car.

I worked the gear shift, got the feel of the synchros and throw from gear to gear. I was a little nervous, the excited case of nerves I get when it's all a game, not like the shakes that run through me when business is serious. A sedan pulled onto the street up ahead, drove toward the condo complex. Its right blinker clicked on, like it was getting ready to turn into the underground garage.

Just what Jerry needed, a car pulling up when he's breaking into the Mercedes. I twisted the ignition, started the engine. The sedan drifted left, veered sharp to the right and spun sideways into the curb six inches from my front bumper. I thought it was trying to duck something crazy coming in the opposite direction, recognised the make too late. Chevy Caprice. My eyes darted to the side mirror. A second sedan slid sideways into the curb just behind me. I was pinned.

I raced the motor, popped the clutch. The van lurched away from the curb, I jerked the wheel hard left. But they had me boxed good. I smashed into the rear fender of the first sedan, jammed into reverse, wrenched the wheel back the other way, but something came up fast from the side and I got hit so hard I lost track of what I was doing.

Next thing I knew there was glass all over, I was being pulled out of the van by my hair, I saw a gun out the corner of my eye and tried to push away but somebody jerked my hands behind my back. I kicked, screamed, tried to run, none of it did any good. They dragged me to the second sedan, threw me head first into the trunk, cracked my skull against the hinges. I twisted around, it was Frick and Frack I saw. Then the trunk slammed shut and I saw nothing at all.

19

No air, no light. We moved fast and steady on a smooth road, had to be a freeway. I kicked, banged my head against the steel side-panels, fighting did me no good at all, just soaked my clothes in sweat. I counted the seconds, the seconds to minutes, took slow deep breaths. It kept my mind from things I didn't want to think about. I didn't want to think about Jerry right then. I asked myself why would he pretend about repossessing the Mercedes. It would be easy to give me up by pulling out his gun, saying here she is.

Counting calmed me. I counted until the car slowed, made a series of turns on what felt like surface streets. They were sure to slap me around some, that's been my experience with men of that type. There was a chance they might kill me when they got what they wanted. I've never been that scared of dying. When it's your time to go, it's your time. But it grated to be pushed over the edge by a couple of assholes.

The sedan coasted up an incline, slowed, inched to

level ground. I heard the driver's door creak open, felt the shocks balance the load shift when the driver stepped out of the car. A key scratched against the lock, the trunk sprung open to the brother who looked a little older, had slivers of gray at his temple. The car had parked in the garage of some house, exposed beams and pitched roof overhead.

The older guy, Frick, he dangled a strip of cloth in front of my face, said, "You try to scream or shout for help, we put this gag over you, understand?"

I got this idea, said, "I don't know how to tell you this. It's a little embarrassing, but my period, it just started."

Frack came up the other side of the car, asked, "What?"

"She says she just started her period."

"It's not too much to ask one of you guys go out and get me something?"

Frack got this weird smile on his face, said, "We like blood."

They pulled me out, walked me into the kind of tract house you find all over Southern California, one-story, wallboard, cheap shag carpet. The door from the garage led to the laundry room, laundry room to kitchen, kitchen to dining room, dining to living room. The house smelled dusty, closed up for months. Paint yellowed and scuffed. The bedrooms were down a long hall. Black-out curtains draped the windows in the back bedroom. Frack shoved me into a wooden chair. Frick cuffed me to the back of it, said, "You thirsty?"

I was. Frick looked at his brother. His brother left the room.

"Cute trick with the dummy case, really fooled us good. It took an hour to get the case back, open it up in good light, discover the switch. You're a smart little girl."

Frack came back with a glass of water, looked at his brother.

Frick said, "Doesn't hurt to be nice. Give it to her."

Frack walked over, threw the water in my face.

Frick said, "What'd you do that for? Now she's all wet."

Frack knelt in front of the chair, slapped me four, five times.

Frick said, "Stop that. Why you hitting her?"

"You said she was wet. I was just drying her off."

"My brother, he gets the weirdest ideas. Dad always said he was a psychopathic son-of-a-bitch but I think it's just he's real creative. One time, there was this guy gave our boss some trouble, tried to run away and hide in Mexico. You know what my brother did?"

"Sent him back across the border, one body part at a time?"

Frick looked like a comedian, just had his punch line shouted out by a heckler.

"How'd you know that?"

"Heard it around."

Frick turned to his brother, said, "Hear that? They're telling stories about you, you're famous." He squatted on his heels, pulled out a handkerchief, wiped the last of the water from my face. He said, "You tell us where the case with the real stuff is, we let you go. It's that simple."

"The police have it."

Frick shook his head, said, "I hear broken bones every time you lie."

"No lie, the police raided the place I was staying this morning, listen to the news if you don't believe me."

"We know about the raid. We have friends. They tell us things, like what the police find and don't."

Frick stood, walked to the door.

I said, "You saying the police didn't find it?"

"I have to make a phone call. You think real hard about telling me the truth when I come back."

When his brother left the room, Frack walked over, shut the door, said, "Fee, fi, fo, fitch, I smell the blood of a lyin' bitch." He walked up close, raised his hand. I flinched, expected to get hit, didn't. He laughed, walked around to the back of the chair. It was worse when I couldn't see him. I heard a soft rustling, couldn't quite place what it was. Moment I figured it out, his fingers ripped at my mouth, shoved a gag down my throat. I tried to spit it out but he tied it in place with a strip of cloth. I screamed. The noise was pitifully small.

He circled the chair, I was powerless to do anything except watch, take it. His fingers unhooked his belt. He had big hands, soft and pink, not the rough, metal-stained hands of my pop. He jerked the belt through the loops, powerful and triumphant, pulling out the belt like he was drawing a sword. I knew the position of the hands, the belt, it was the perspective caused me to remember, looking level at his waist, same height as a child. Not a rape gesture. Not yet. Just a whipping.

He folded the belt in half, tip to buckle, snapped the leather across the back of the chair. I wasn't going to look at him, cry out in pain if I could help it. I was going to stare straight ahead and take it. He teased me with the belt at first, slapped it gently over my shoulders. I was food, my fear fed him. The slaps stopped being so gentle. The snap of leather cut deeper until it wasn't a sting anymore, but the sharp pain of being hacked to pieces. His breathing was fast and hard as he worked me over. He arched high on his toes before lashing down. His face was blood-red. Sweat flew off him as he struck. I looked up at him just once, recognized nothing human. He was like a hyena going after meat, gorging itself all jaws and frenzy.

I shrunk myself down as small and hard as I could, let everything go except this one secret place I have to hide. He couldn't get to me in there. The pain was fierce, but it was happening to somebody else's body. I knew how to shrink down to a nut-hard core, where the pain couldn't get to me as much, where I could be strong and hard. My body was just this sack of flesh surrounding me. He could do whatever he wanted to it. Fuck it. Cut it. Kill it. Didn't matter. He couldn't get to me through my body. It seemed like I always knew how to hide myself. There was always this last refuge when things got bad.

Then the hitting stopped. I knew it would. The hitting always stopped, eventually. A hand softly slapped my cheek, untied the strip of cloth, pulled the gag out of my mouth. I heard the creak of a hinge as the door opened, smelled cigarette smoke.

Frick stepped into the room, asked, "Wait a minute, why you crying'?"

"I think I scare her," Frack answered.

"Is that it? Does he scare you?"

Frick's voice was calm and soothing, like a daddy.

I couldn't make my mouth work, was too far inside myself. I stuttered, not getting any words out, just syllables, finally pushed it through clenched teeth that he hit me.

He said, "I told you not to hit her."

"Hey, I didn't hit her that hard, not any harder than when you were here, anyway. She's just a crybaby."

Frick dropped his hand on my shoulder. I flinched. He

said I shouldn't be afraid of him, he didn't want to hurt me, he was sorry if something bad happened while he was away. His brother was a little crazy, couldn't always control him. I lied, said I wasn't afraid, it was just that he put his hand on a sore spot where I'd been whipped. Then he noticed the welts on my neck where the belt hit me.

Frick pulled his brother over, said, "Did you do that?"

"Maybe," Frack answered.

"I told you not to."

"I got inspired."

Frick knelt in front of me again, tried to look in my eyes, said, "You see what I'm talking about? My brother, he's a real pain artist. When he gets creative, he has a mind of his own. Long as I stay here, you don't have to worry."

I knew this guy was not my friend any more than Frack was. They were playing a game with me. I couldn't help believing him. It was so damn seductive, his concern for me after I'd been beaten. Like I expected to get love after pain. They were somehow the same for me. Like there was something I couldn't quite remember that fused the two together so long ago I couldn't feel one without the other. I let my head rest against his hand.

Frick stroked my hair, said, "It tears my heart out to leave you alone again, afraid what my brother might do.

Can you please just tell me where that case is? Once we find it, why, we can let you go."

"I got no reason to lie, you guys are crazy killing each other over a stupid toilet, I left it in the studio, it was there yesterday."

"That doesn't do us any good, to hear that."

"It's what happened."

"Now I gotta go out looking for it, leave you alone here with my brother. Scares me just thinking about what could happen."

I choked up, said, "I got two room-mates, maybe one of them took it."

"Took it where?"

I thought about Billy b. It wasn't him sitting in this chair, getting hit, sure, he betrayed me, deserved what he got. I said, "Try SMART Gallery, in Santa Monica."

"You don't sound very sure."

"It's the only thing I can think happened to it."

"This is a problem," Frick said, his voice heavy and sad. "Because we need to get it back now. You took us someplace, said, here it is, then we could let you go. We don't have the time to go searching through half the city for a couple of room-mates."

I knew what the regret in his voice meant, that I was going to get another beating because I hadn't told him what he wanted to know. He shrugged like he was real sorry about it. His brother leaned against the bureau, stared with cold hunger at an invisible mark six inches above my head. I said I couldn't help it, I was telling the truth, I even begged him to stay, but all he said was he had to go make another call.

I knew pain was coming. I expected his brother to use the belt again. I wasn't going to plead with him any more than I would a beast eating me alive, just pretend I was dead and hope he lost interest. He said he was going to show what happened to bitches that lie, but I didn't care what he said or did. He had me in his physical power, and there was nothing I could do about it except not let him break me. I told myself I will survive this, and though I would have blasted the asshole to hell in a second if I had the chance, I wasn't thinking of physical revenge. I was thinking survival will be my revenge. He will not get to me. There are places I can hide where he will never find me.

Frack pried my mouth open, stuffed the gag down my throat, tied it in place with the strip of cloth. It was like he was doing it to somebody else. I watched it all from a perch in the corner of the room. If he thought that was me hurting, that was me crying, he was wrong. That wasn't me. He didn't have any idea I was watching him from up there, near the ceiling. He thought I was still in my body. He knelt in front of me. A pack of wooden matches came out of his pocket, then a cigarette. The bright ripping sound of sulfur flared out. My eyes tracked the fire as it ignited the tobacco and left the tip. He touched the match to the wisps of hair hanging from my forehead. They went up in flame. I squirmed and bucked. He grabbed my hair to stop me moving, hovered the coal of his cigarette a quarter inch away from the inside of my wrist. The skin smoldered and burned. He stabbed out the coal in my flesh, tossed the butt to the floor. He lit a second cigarette and smoked for a while, watched me, crushed the second cigarette out a little higher up my arm. He smoked half a pack that way.

I don't want to talk about it anymore.

The scars aren't so bad. It's not like I'm horribly disfigured or anything. Like most scars, with a little cosmetics, nobody notices. If I wear a long-sleeve shirt with a high collar, nobody even has to know the scars are there. See, nothing wrong with me. Good as new. The scars will shrink and fade, blend with the slow ruin of my skin. Maybe in twenty years or so, the traces will vanish from my flesh, until all that remains is the lingering memory of pain.

A can pressed cool and moist into the palm of my hand. A voice told me to drink. I drank, couldn't get more than a couple swallows down. I wanted to believe the pain would not get any worse. Some new horror was not ready to hammer down, scatter my self-resistance like a smashed walnut. The voice talked about something, I couldn't make sense of what. A hand slapped at mine, moved the can to my lips. I took another swallow, forced it down, saw it was Frick, he was back, he was talking, it was coke he'd given me. He pronounced his words careful and slow, said he just got back from talking with the boss, personally he thought I was being sincere, but his boss thought I was stalling for time. I must have forgot something. Was there anything else I could add, something he could tell his boss, so they could find the case sooner? That way, we wouldn't have to worry about his brother anymore. He could let me go.

I said if he wanted to hear lies, leave me alone with his brother again. I'd make up all kinds of shit. I'd do anything they wanted. Tell the truth. Lie. Anything. Because I just couldn't take the pain anymore, my period was starting, I felt sick to my stomach, if he had human feeling he'd let me use the bathroom.

Frick said, "Fine, you need to use the bathroom, why didn't you say so in the first place? We're not criminals here. I don't like this situation any more than you do. All you have to do is ask."

I waited for him to unlock the handcuffs from the chair, but he just looked at me. His brother laughed. They wanted to hear me ask to use the bathroom. He wanted me a little girl, asking permission, wanted me humiliated. Little girls raise their hands, ask to be excused. That was what he wanted, dominance and humiliation. He was saying, you can't do anything without me. I control your body, I control your mind.

I broke into tears, asked him, "Could I please go to the bathroom?"

He was sure he had me then.

"Of course," he said.

The right handcuff snapped off, the left stayed on my wrist. Frick helped me onto my feet, guided me out of the bedroom to the bathroom in the hall. He stroked my hair as we walked, said "There, there, little girl, it's okay. I'll take good care of you."

"You want to take good care of me, send your brother to the drugstore, okay?"

I stepped into the bathroom, started to close the door.

He stopped me, asked, "Aren't you forgetting something?"

I asked him what, confused, because I didn't know what he was talking about. He reached down to touch my handcuffs. I got it. I was supposed to volunteer to have the cuffs put on again. I extended my hands, said, "I'm sorry, but can I please have my hands in front, so I can, you know, take care of myself better?"

"I don't see why not. But you promise to be good now?"

I promised. He latched the cuffs in front, shut the door behind me. I bolted for the toilet, threw up. I felt a little better after that, but it wasn't the food in my stomach making me sick. It was the humiliation making me sick. I stood at the sink to wash out my mouth. My skin was ghost white.

I said, "Hey, ho, it's only rock and roll."

Cold water trickled over the burn on my wrist. The sting dulled. I plugged up the sink, filled it with cold water, plunged in my arms. The water covered the burns below my elbows, made the burns above water seem even hotter. Better than nothing, gave me a little quiet time to think.

I thought about Frick. He wanted to fuck me. Maybe I'd guessed wrong, blood turned him on. He didn't want it to be rape. He wanted me dependent, wanted me to want it. I told myself no way, never would I want to sleep with him. But I knew I was lying to myself. It was already happening. Abuse and dependency. Can't have one without the other. I grew up in a situation made me an expert in seeing it happen, only I didn't always know when it was happening to me. The little lies start first. He really cares or he's different or he's the one gonna save me. It's easy to believe when belief is all you have. No way Frick gave a shit about me. He could fuck me one day, kill me the next, sleep just fine the night after.

I guess I'm pretty fucked up. It's strange to think I'm fucked up, because I always wanted to be not just normal, but super normal. The one person didn't have any problems. The one you could talk to, could always depend on. I think it was because I could hide better that way. If I acted like everything was okay, then it was okay. But now, when I think about it, I guess I am pretty fucked up about things.

I opened the medicine cabinet and checked under the sink, tried to find some kind of weapon I could use. A bar of soap in the shower, an old toothbrush in the medicine cabinet, a towel hanging from a hook on the door. The bathroom was pretty much stripped. I soaked the towel in cold water, wrung halfway it out, wrapped it around my left arm, the burned one. It was a trick working around the handcuffs. I tied the ends together with my teeth.

Behind the door, Frick called, "You didn't fall in, now did you?"

I jumped hearing his voice, shouted, "I'm fine."

"I want you out of there in two minutes, y'got that?"

I bit my tongue to keep from saying, *Yes, daddy*.

The toothbrush looked dirty, the bristles splayed and ratty. I scrubbed the bristles on the bar of soap, brushed my teeth. Five or six mouthfuls of warm water rinsed out the taste of soap. I rapped the toothbrush against the sink to shake it out. The toothbrush was a clear-blue plastic Oral B. Ridges cut halfway up the handle, where the thumb goes when somebody holds it. Above the ridges, the handle slanted in to form a long neck, then out again at the head, which held the bristles. I gave the toothbrush a wrench, snapped off the head at the neck. I was trying to get the neck to shatter lengthwise, form a tapered knife edge. No luck. But the edge was jagged enough to do some damage. I slipped the handle between my skin and the towel, dropped the severed bristles into the toilet, flushed, opened the bathroom door.

Frick was there, waiting.

I said, "I look like shit, don't I?"

I hoped like hell he wouldn't notice the missing toothbrush, he'd think I wasn't capable of trying anything, I was just a dumb girl worried how good she looked on her way to the grave.

He glanced around the bathroom, said, "You look just great."

His hands wrapped around the towel at my forearm, squeezed.

"What's this?"

I flinched away, said the burns hurt bad, the cool water in the towel made them feel better.

He looked at me sharply, thought it through, said, "I had a burn once, hurt like a son-of-a-bitch. The only thing to make it better was cold water and a half pint of Stolichnaya."

"You have any vodka? 'Cause a little sure would taste good right now."

He smiled, happy to give a little pleasure after big pain, said, "I don't see why not, a little vodka can't hurt. But you have to understand, I can't let you drink more than a little."

"Any chance I can get some fresh clothes, a little make-up so I can look halfway decent?"

He lit up hearing me say that. I didn't want to push it. Not then. I could feel him wanting me, that sixth sexual sense I sometimes have, knowing what a guy is thinking if he's thinking about me. He sat me down, cuffed my wrists to the chair, whispered he'd be back with that vodka in just a minute.

I listened hard to the sounds in the house, wanted to

know for sure his brother was gone. I heard Frick clattering in the kitchen. Nothing else. Not that it meant anything. His brother could still be somewhere inside. It worried me, because I didn't know what I was doing but I had to do it or die trying. White noise started coming up in my brain. I closed my eyes and breathed, fought the blankness, made an imaginary movie about what I had to do. Imagine it, make it happen.

Frick stroked the palm of my hand with the key, smirked, unlocked the cuff from the chair, it dangled from my right wrist, left both hands free. I smiled for him. He held a bottle of vodka wasn't Stolichnaya, it was some off-brand, a big bottle with a little price. But it was clear and eighty proof and vodka is vodka. He produced two paper cups, said, "You didn't think I was gonna give you glass, something you could use to hit me with?"

I shook my head, held out the paper cup. He teased the bottom with a splash, laughed when I shook the cup for more. I tossed it down without a taste, held out the cup for a refill.

"Like to drink do you?" he said, and gave me another splash. "I think we're going to get along just fine. I like a girl likes to drink."

I sipped the vodka carefully, said, "I like strong men, always have. My Pop, he was strong, so I guess I got used to it early."

Frick gave me another splash of vodka, enjoyed measuring it out drop by drop, said, "Then it looks like we're gonna like each other."

He inched forward, like he was getting ready to test just how much we liked each other. I raised the cup to my lips to slow him down, asked, "You like working for this Fleischer guy?"

"Sure, Fleischer is smart, we're all gonna make a fortune on this deal. You have any idea what's in that case?"

I said, "Not a clue."

"I don't either, to me it's just a toilet, but Fleischer, he's smart, to him it's art, big money, millions."

"Killing Kabyenko, seems pretty stupid."

"Kabyenko knew where it came from, the thing is worth a ton long as nobody knows it's stolen, he could step in at any moment and fuck the whole million-dollar deal, no way we could risk that."

I said, "Oh."

Frick said, "I know what you're thinking, you know where it came from, we'll kill you too. But you're with me, I like you."

I held out my glass for another shot of vodka, smiled for him.

He said, "You're trembling."

I was, and bad. I saw a flicker of doubt in his eyes, a dimwitted sensation that something was wrong. I had to say something. I had to act. I told him something close enough to the truth to pass for it. I said, "I'm scared, don't know what's happening to me."

"You'll be alright, little girl. I'll take good care of you."

I looked up into his eyes, let him see the hurt I was feeling and a little bit of the true wanting. I said, "Just hold me."

It was what he wanted, what he planned all along. I was giving it to him. I was asking for it. He wrapped his arms around my waist and shoulders. I buried my face in his neck, let the cup fall to the floor. The machinery of arousal geared through his body. Muscles stiffened, flexed, hips began to move. I turned my face, let him kiss me. A little cry escaped my lips. He thought it was passion, but it was the pain of what I was doing. I dropped my hand from his shoulder while he kissed me, the worm-like wriggling of his tongue inside my mouth, and drew the broken toothbrush from underneath the towel.

I closed the kiss and pushed him back with my mouth, the way you do when the kiss is ended and you don't want another one. There was a determined hunger in his face then, the kind of look on the face of a dog pushed from the dinner bowl. He was confused why I pushed him away, strained to come back for more. But when he saw my eyes, he knew something was wrong.

I shot the handle straight toward his throat, it caught

him just above the Adam's apple. He roared and fell
back, ripped from the center of his throat up to his ear. I
grabbed the chair, lifted it over my head, swung down.
He got his shoulder up, deflected the blow. I raised the
chair again, but he recovered fast, kicked the legs out
from under me. I rolled onto my feet, kicked him along
the side of his head as he was trying to get up. It stunned
him, but he got to his feet, stood between me and the
door. My only chance was to put him out. I went for the
chair.

He saw what I wanted to do but couldn't get there fast
enough to stop me. I swung the chair by its feet. He
hunched his head down and took it on his shoulders, the
chair wrenched from my hands on impact. Nothing left
between him and me except carpet and a lot of hostility.
He threw a right. I ducked, went for his balls with my
knee. He twisted aside, swung his elbow like a club into
my jaw. I fell back, lashed out with the cuffs, tried to cut
him. He blocked it easy, countered with a shot just about
broke my ribs. I doubled up hurt like hell and thought,
shit, I'd missed everything, his windpipe, his artery, his
head, my chance. He cocked his fist back like he was
going to chop down, put my lights out for good. I charged
straight into him, spun away, bolted for the door. His fist
slammed against my neck and I went crashing into the
bureau.

The lamp hit the floor, the light-bulb blew and sucked

the light out of the room. I crawled for the line of light at the base of the door. Frick jumped on me from behind, pushed my face into the carpet. I bucked hard as I could, got nowhere. He weighed about two hundred pounds, no way was I going to budge him. I had to keep my arms free, reached out to grab a leg of the bureau, couldn't stretch far enough, get a grip on it. His hand clamped down on mine, jerked it behind my back. The shoulder socket started to strip out like a chicken wing. I screamed in pain, he gave an extra jerk for good measure, said, "Like that, little girl?"

I clawed at the carpet, tried to inch up and ease the pressure, but he caught my free hand at the thumb, twisted it behind my back. The cuffs snapped shut around my wrists. He squirmed up my body, whispered I was a liar, I'd lied about the case and lied about feeling sick and probably lied about my period, too. Maybe it would take him time to learn the truth about the case, but about my period, he could find out if I was lying about that right away, couldn't he? I felt his hands digging under my stomach, going for my belt. I screamed at him to stop or I swore I'd kill him. He clipped the side of my head, said, "You wanna talk about killing, little girl? I'll show you killing."

I screamed and bucked. He dug his elbow into my neck so I couldn't twist my head, it hurt like hell but I kicked anyway. He couldn't get my belt undone with me fighting him. He wrapped his forearm around my throat and squeezed. I started to pass out. He told me not to fight, just lie back and enjoy it. When I came to again, he had my belt off, was trying to rip my jeans over my hips.

The sound of an opening door stopped him. I heard it too, coming from the front of the house. Frick tensed, scrambled to his knees. Maybe he wasn't supposed to be doing this to me, was afraid what his brother would think. I could see him out the corner of my eye, listening. He jumped to his feet, his hand went to the gash on his neck.

He called out, "Frack? That you, Frack?"

Nobody answered.

Frick opened the door, craned a look down the hall. The air ripped apart with a ragged blast, he lurched back like somebody hit him. The door frame stopped him from falling. He steadied himself against it, then stood his ground, like he didn't believe he'd just been shot. Another bullet tore out, all noise and fury, he went down every muscle gone at the same time. His leg trembled for a couple seconds after he fell, but that was all. It was scary watching him drop, how quickly he'd been sucked out to darkness. The leg stilled and the only thing about him that moved was his blood spreading a dark red stain in the carpet.

Boots thumped down the hall. I thought it had to be Jerry. He didn't Judas me after all. He saw I was kidnapped, now he's come to rescue me. A pair of blue-jeaned legs crossed the doorway into the room, but the boots were wrong, not the lizard-skin Tony Lamas Jerry wore, but black lace-up Doc Martens.

A voice said, "Hey, babe, good to see ya."

Wrex's voice.

Wrex took the key off Frick's body, unlocked the cuffs, suggested we motor, because of the sound of the gun and all. He wrapped his bandanna bandit-style across his face, told me not to show my face until we were on the road. I followed him to the door, stopped short. I asked to see his gun for a second. He wanted to know what for. I told him don't argue, just give me the gun. He did. I checked the safety like Jerry taught me, pumped three bullets into Frick's dead body.

"Rest in pieces, asshole," I said.

21

The stars were out, the desert freeway clear of traffic. Wrex took advantage, let the Harley run. I held on tight, wrapped in Wrex's leather jacket, the bike charging between my legs. Dawn stoked the eastern horizon. I breathed in the desert, felt a momentary freedom, like a prisoner finds a vein of fresh air, closes her eyes, imagines no walls around.

We rode an hour and a half straight, got into Hollywood as the first brutal rays of sun speared over the hills. I told Wrex I had to eat something. He pulled into the parking lot of Ben Franks, an all-night coffee shop on Sunset Boulevard famous for years to insomniacs and graveyarders and druggies. There was a corner booth free. I took it. Wrex hid behind his black Ray-Bans, raised a menu soon as he sat, pretended nothing was wrong. I told him what I wanted, curled up in his jacket to nod out a minute on the seat cushion. Something hard in one of the pockets dug into my ribs. I reached to shift it around. My fingers brushed against the curve of a trigger guard. It was the gun. I fumbled for the safety, made sure it was on, pulled the jacket around so the barrel pointed away from me, went instantly asleep.

I had no dreams. Just a deep fall into darkness felt like death. When the food arrived Wrex pulled me into a sitting position over the table. Felt like dirt in my joints, bones sticking through my skin, parts of my brain rotted away. A cup of coffee slid under my nose. The smell of caffeine was a trickle of electricity in my nostrils. I gripped the eating utensils and forked down some egg, a bite of hash-browns, a hunk of ham, discovered I was incredibly hungry, my sole purpose in life condensed to getting the food on my plate into my mouth, chewed, shoved down to my stomach.

When I finished eating, I said to Wrex, "Take off your sunglasses."

He dutifully jammed the sunglasses into the front pocket of his t-shirt, asked if I was happy now, just a little sarcasm in his voice.

"Anything wrong with me wanting to see your eyes?"

He raised his big browns all innocent to meet mine, gave me a look made him seem vulnerable and cute. It wasn't the time for me to go soft.

I asked, "What the hell were you trying to do?"

"Do?" he answered, just a little confused.

"You know what I'm talking about."

But Wrex didn't know. I looked for guilt in his expression, didn't find any. Not that it fooled me. Sometimes what looks like a clear conscience is just a blank brain. I said, "What happened about two weeks ago, made me a fugitive?"

"I didn't know the damn thing was going to explode! You think I'da had anything to do with this if I knew there was a bomb in that case?"

I stared him straight in the face, nodded.

That hit Wrex hard. His voice turned hurt. He said, "Then I guess we got nothing to say to each other."

He stared out the window, eyes misting up like he was going to cry any second. Waited for me to say something. I let him wait. I was about feeling sorry for him when he turned from the window, said, "That's the thanks I get for saving your life. Makes me wonder why I did it."

"Okay. Why'dja do it?"

"Do what?"

"Save me."

"Babe, I been tryin' to find you for two weeks."

"I ask because it's obvious the only person you care about is yourself."

"But, babe, you're the one I love."

"You love something outside yourself, it's your bike."

"When you get like this, it's like tryin' to talk to a

scorpion. Everything I say, your tail comes up and you try to sting me to death."

I said, "Fine, go ahead and explain."

"You have to believe I didn't know anything about this."

"I don't have to believe anything."

"The Drake brothers told me nothing about any bomb."

"Just said you shouldn't stick around."

"Didn't say that at all."

"If you did, expect a sudden one-way flight through the roof."

"Said it was completely legal what we were doing."

"Liar."

"If I'm such a bad guy, what am I doing here? Why didn't I just leave you with the Drakes?"

That was a no-brainer, even for me.

"Because you want the case, and you think I got it."

Wrex gawked at me, dumbfounded, or maybe just dumb.

I said, "Direct hit, huh?"

"The Drake brothers were tryin' to whack me. Like it was good ol' Wrex's fault you absconded off! I say that makes us equal."

"Equal how?"

"Equal partners. What's in that thing, anyway?"

"You wouldn't believe if I told you."

"I say we give it back."

I looked at him like, who are you trying to fool, but the weird thing was, he seemed really sincere, didn't have that glazed-over look his eyes get when he lies. I said, "Explain what you mean by give."

"Give like in give back."

"You never gave anything away in your life. Why start now?"

"I'm still in love, babe. Maybe even more now. I mean, you were okay as a blonde, but now, with your hair chopped like that, and your nose pierced and everything, you look really hot."

All this time he was pouring his big browns over me like honey, and even though just yesterday "Wrex" and "asshole" were synonyms in my vocabulary, there was something about him that got to me. But it wasn't love, it was hormones, it made me mad that all he had to do was look at me a certain way and they started stirring again. I said, "I have one t-shirt, one pair of jeans, one bra, and one pair of underwear which I swear I haven't washed in a week, so don't talk to me about hot."

Wrex reached across the table, cupped my hands.

I couldn't help it. I smiled.

He said, "C'mon, babe, let's go somewhere where we can, you know, be alone."

"You want to make love now, after all that's happened?"

He thought about it a second, said, "Well, yeah."

I jerked my hands away.

"So what's wrong with that?"

"A million years, Wrex. The space of time between now and when the dinosaurs roamed the earth. That's how long it's gonna be before our private parts ever touch again."

"What I mean to say is . . ." he started, and his eyes shifted back and forth while he tried to think just what it was he meant to say. "I love you," came his final declaration. "And whatever you decide to do and all, well, I'll stick by you."

I was not one hundred per cent crazy about having Wrex stick by me, or stick to me, depending how I interpreted his motivations. I sipped coffee and stared out the window for a while, wondered what the hell I was going to do now.

Wrex said, "You know, sooner or later we'll both end up in jail. I mean, you killed somebody. Two people are dead 'cause of this. I don't think the pigs are just gonna forget that."

I told him thanks, I could count up to two all by myself, the way I looked at it, neither of the two were worth losing any sleep over.

"Well, babe, I think that's right, but what I'm tryin' to say here is, there might be another way to go about things."

"Yeah? What."

"Just that you're gonna give that thing away and go to jail for a hundred long hard years, when you might just as easy let me give it back for you, and with my negotiating skills, maybe get a little something for it, enough to get to Mexico until things cool down a little here."

"I'm not selling the case, Wrex."

"I'm not talkin' about selling it. Just getting our aggravation money back."

"You going to get them to sign something says the money isn't for dealing in stolen property, it's some kinda fee for interrupted lifestyle? That's one weird moral distinction, even for you."

"Morals got nothing to do with it. I can get fifty grand for what's in that case."

"Who you gonna give it back to?" I asked, suddenly afraid we were talking about giving the thing back to different parties.

"To the suit who hired the Drake brothers, that's who."

I stripped Wrex's jacket off, handed it to him as I walked away from the table. Said thanks for saving my life, thanks for breakfast. He shouted I should wait, but there was no stopping me. I was out the door and walking along Sunset Boulevard, suddenly wondering where I was going to go. Because I had no place, nobody.

A block up Sunset, Wrex coasted to the curb beside me, revved his bike to keep from stalling out, said, "C'mon, babe, hop on."

I didn't cut him so much as a look.

"You do what you want with the case. I said I was gonna stick by you, and I meant it."

I shouted, "I don't know where it is!"

"What?"

"The case! I left it someplace, and it disappeared. I don't know where the case is, understand?"

Wrex's eyes went dead for a second and that told me all I really needed to know. He wrenched down on the throttle, dropped the Harley into gear, and the noise of the bike ripping away from the curb shook windows, rattled cups for miles around.

To hell with him. It was just hormones. I didn't even like him. He was dumb as a stone, had all the future of one falling off a cliff. It figured all he wanted was the case. I was angry at myself as much as him, because I kept falling for the same old things. What I couldn't understand was how he could say one thing with his eyes while his brain was thinking completely different. When he stared at me with his big brown eyes, I thought I could see all the way down to his heart, and his heart was saying he loved me. One of the reasons I fell for him. Big reason. But there was something alien, or maybe just male, about his brain. How he felt never interfered with how he thought, and it was his brain that mostly decided how to react to things.

I heard his bike roar up behind me a second time. I turned to look at him. He had a big grin on his face, shouted over the bike noise, "Bet I fooled you that time. Bet you thought I was really gone."

I hauled off, slugged him as hard as I could on the arm.

He said, "C'mon, babe, don't fight me."

I hopped on the back of his bike, held on to him from behind as he accelerated into traffic, pressed my face against the hot leather at his back. The wind flayed the burns on my arms, but I didn't care. It was good to have a body to hold on to. Maybe Wrex had his faults, but he did come back for me, didn't he?

I yelled above the bike roar I wanted him to take me downtown, near San Pedro, to a loft I knew about, did he mind? He wrenched back on the throttle, threaded the dotted line between lanes, took Sunset Boulevard to the Hollywood Freeway. I could use Wrex to get a message to Cass, find out what was happening. I got lost thinking, didn't pay attention where he was going. He got off the freeway too soon, shouted he wanted to take surface streets. I took him at his word, didn't worry. The direction was good, toward San Pedro, somewhere in Little Tokyo he leaned sharply, turned the bike into an underground garage. I looked up to see where we were.

I recognised the building. Same building Fleischer Security Systems was in.

I yelled, "What the hell you doing?"

Wrex skirted the barrier at the ticket machine, accelerated down the parking ramp. I was afraid he was going to lay the bike down the way he leaned into the first corner, but he pulled the bike up at the last instant and blistered past an aisle of cars toward the next ramp, winding down the subterranean levels to where lot density would thin to a car or two. To a place of no witnesses. I held on tight, lost my concentration against the speed and blast of bike noise bouncing off concrete walls. My arm pressed against something hard at his side as I held on, took me just a second to realize Wrex left the gun in his jacket pocket.

The bike straightened coming out of a turn. I snaked my right hand into the jacket pocket and grabbed the butt. Wrex clamped his elbow down, pinned my wrist to his ribs before I could pull the gun free. But to do that he had to let go of the throttle, steer the bike with one hand. A corner came up too fast to stop. He had to let go of my wrist or lay the bike down. His hand bolted for the throttle. I jerked out the gun. When we leaned into the curve, the rear wheel started to slide out.

I pushed hard on Wrex's back as the bike started to go, didn't want to get caught between the ground and red-hot pipes. My hip hit the concrete. I lost the gun curling up my arms to protect my head. After the first bounce I slid clean, burned through my jeans at the hip, skidded under the bumper of a parked pickup truck and slammed into the tire. For a moment, I wasn't anywhere, didn't think or feel anything.

Wrex screamed horribly somewhere on the other side of the truck. I couldn't see him, felt a wave of panic he was seriously hurt. From under the pickup I could see the bike was down on the other side. But he wasn't down with it. Then I saw his legs. Vertical. Walking toward his bike. He screamed again. It was his Harley he was screaming about. Typical Wrex. I pulled myself out from under the truck and sat up, counted body parts.

Wrex called, "That you, babe?"

I didn't answer.

His boots scuffed on concrete, like he was walking in circles.

"You still got the gun?"

Oh yeah. The gun. I slid onto my stomach as quiet as I could, looked around ground level. It took me a moment to spot it, lying against the wall in front of the pickup truck. I could see his legs on the other side, turning circles. He wasn't looking for me. He was looking for the gun. I pushed myself up to a crouch, scrambled toward the wall.

Wrex heard me move. When I cleared the front

bumper of the pickup, he was coming from the other side. He saw the gun and dove, both feet going horizontal as he sprawled out for it. I was on top of the gun before his body hit the ground. I grabbed it around the cylinder, jumped to my feet. He clutched at my ankles to trip me up but I kicked him away, pointed the barrel at his head, hoped he'd take the hint and chill out.

Wrex favored his left leg as he struggled to his knees. His jeans were all ripped up, I could see he'd got a bad case of road burn. He hunched his shoulders, sighed and shook his head, met the eye of the gun with a sad stare.

"Go ahead. Shoot me down like a dog. I guess you think I deserve it."

"I wouldn't shoot a dog, but I just might shoot you, because you're lower than a dog. At least a dog won't turn on you if it's your friend."

I shook the gun at him like it was a finger while I talked, and this made sweat-balls of worry drip down his forehead, because I was putting considerable pressure on the trigger.

He said, "You wanna watch out for that thing, 'cause it's loaded."

I centered the sights between his eyes, held the gun steady, said, "Safety's off, too. Already checked."

He tried to laugh, couldn't, said, "I have a friend in

this building, that's all. We were in the neighborhood, so why not stop by?"

"Your friend, he wouldn't happen to be named Mike Fleischer?"

Wrex smiled the same time his eyes glazed over. He pushed himself up off the bumper of the pick-up truck, said, "C'mon, babe, just talk to the guy is all I ask. He's not going to gangst you. He's a suit. What's wrong with talking to him? He'll give us some money, and I can go to Mexico."

"You can go to Mexico? What about me?"

Wrex thought about it for a second, one second too long as far as I was concerned. He stepped forward, tried to close the distance between us, said, "Well, you can go to Mexico, too." The way he said it, I didn't feel included in his plans, like maybe I'd get in his way with the senoritas. He realized he hadn't quite sold me on the idea, because that was the moment I cocked the hammer back with my thumb.

"Of course I meant together. You and me. White sands, tequila, warm sunshine, and the fish, why they'll practically leap onto the grill!"

He took another step forward, whispered, "Ten thousand dollars!"

I backed toward the corner.

"Just to talk to him!"

"You were selling me out, Wrex."

"Babe! Never!" He stepped forward again, forced my back against the wall. "I was going to be there the whole time. I had a gun. I mean, why not talk to him?"

I said, "One step more, and I swear to God I'll shoot you."

Wrex looked at me, the gun, and the five-foot gap that separated us like it was a one-way drop to hell between him and heaven. But he started to think, and for Wrex thinking was dangerous, it put him one foot in never-never land. I could tell what he was thinking. I was having some of the same thoughts myself. About how completely absurd it was that I was going to shoot him, Wrex, a guy I'd slept with, thought I loved. I felt the revolver wobble in my hands. He took it as a sign, walked toward me, said, "Come on, babe."

I told him to stop, and he didn't, he took another step forward, reached out his hand. I thought about what he'd done to me. The bomb in the airport, selling me out to Fleischer. It made me mad. I pulled the trigger. I shot him.

Wrex staggered back, said, "You bitch!"

I said I was sorry, but I'd warned him.

Wrex glanced down at his leg. The bullet had pierced mid-way between his and knee. He clutched above the wound, cried, "You fucking shot me!"

I felt no remorse. I said, "I was aiming six inches higher and more toward the center. Get my point?"

His knees went rubbery, he dropped on his butt, sounded pitiful when he said, "Don't let me die here."

I set the gun out of reach, told him if he tried any physical stuff I'd shoot him again. He said he wasn't going to do anything to hurt me, I had him all wrong, he never wanted to hurt me. I didn't see any bones sticking out, there was blood but it wasn't like somebody turned on the tap full blast. I stripped the bandanna off his head and cinched it down hard above the wound. His leather jacket was about to get blood on it, so I pulled it off his back. Couldn't see what good it was doing him. He started to protest when I put it on. I jammed the revolver into the jacket pocket and zipped up, said I was going to get him an ambulance, didn't want to freeze.

He said, "You shot me, and now you wanna rip off my leather jacket?"

I said, "That's right, I shot you, I ripped off your jacket, next I'm going to steal your bike."

I walked over to his Harley. It was scraped and dinged on the left side, but started just fine. Wrex yelled all kinds of evil opinions about my character while I checked out the gears. He crawled desperately toward the bike, his shot leg trailing behind, and when he noticed his threats weren't cutting it with me, he pleaded I could do anything, I could shoot him in the arm if I wanted, just don't steal his bike. The Harley was a big bike, bigger than anything I ever rode before. My feet didn't reach the ground. I had to lean the bike and prop it up with one foot. Made starts and stops difficult, which is why I ran Wrex over when I accidentally popped the clutch and roared off. I wasn't trying to run him down. He'd crawled in front of the bike. All the months we were going out together he never let me ride solo. It was his fault as much as mine I hit him. If he'd taught me how to ride the thing in the first place, or just stayed put, I never would have broke his other leg.

I rode the Harley into Hollywood, parked it around the block from Ben's office, walked to my truck. A pink parking ticket fluttered in wind. The fine was twenty-six bucks. I tore it up, threw the pieces on to the passenger seat. So arrest me. I cranked up the mini-truck. The tank was a quarter full. First law of LA, if there's gas, there's hope.

I drove out to Venice, ditched the revolver in the springs under the seat, got out of the truck, walked to the beach. People stared out the corner of turned-away faces as I walked by. I had some blood on me from where the concrete scraped away parts of my hip and elbow. My hands were red with Wrex's blood. The one knee of my jeans was soaked where I'd knelt in a pool of it, tying the tourniquet around his leg. I didn't worry much how I looked. Nobody was going to call the police because it seemed like I was having a tough time. Venice Beach looked to be full of people just as down on their luck as me, probably had stories even crazier than the one I was living. If somebody called about me, they'd have to call about the other twenty thousand homeless people on the streets looked just as bad or worse. I moved along like it was the most normal thing in the world, like this was my own peculiar reality I was living, nothing for anybody else to worry about.

I walked into the ocean, ducked under the waves, let the water rush blue-white-green over my head. The saltwater stung my cuts and burns. Out over the water, a solitary pelican skimmed the waves, beak-heavy and awkward. With a shift of wing, the bird banked toward open sea. I closed my eyes, pretended I was her, just flying away from it all. A wave crashed overhead, pulled me back down. I sat in the froth, scrubbed the blood off my hands with coarse, wet sand. When the blood was gone, I walked up to where the sand was dry, fell asleep.

My eyes opened to a tongue of sea-water lapping my feet. I sat up, watched the wild curl and claw of high tide, thought about things. A couple weeks before, I imagined a new life for myself, a complete break with the old notions of who I was, what I wanted. It hadn't worked. I escaped nothing. I should have given myself up the day the bomb exploded. Should have been a good girl, gone straight to the police, told them, *Look, I got a stupid job and screwed-up family and car payments. I perm my hair, paint my toenails pink, wear fuzzy knit sweaters. I'm a solid citizen, so normal it hurts. It was my boyfriend did it. Black leather, rides a Harley, a terrorist if you ever saw one. I'm a victim of bad influences.* I never should have bolted with this wild idea I could change. I should have stayed sleeping in my safe little world. Maybe I was happier sleeping. Sleeping passes the time so you don't know where you are, what problems you have.

The ocean breeze chilled me. I got up, thought I'd walk myself dry. I walked up to Main Street, found a phone booth, got the number for SMART Gallery, dialed it. A receptionist answered. I told her I was Cass, had to talk to Billy b, was he there? She said she thought he was going to be back in an hour or so, did I want to leave a message? Then I called Ben.

I said, "Hey, Ben, seen Jerry around?"

"Is he pissed at you."

"What'd I do?"

"Said you smashed up his van and ran off. Couldn't find you anywhere."

I didn't know if I wanted to believe that or not. I asked, "You got any friends with the police?"

Ben said, "You don't have to worry about him pressing charges."

"This is about something else."

"You in trouble?"

"Uh-huh."

"Bad trouble?"

"Depends on how you feel about the electric chair."

There was silence on the other end.

I said, "I need you to help me. I'll drop by the office, say before midnight. You mind staying late?"

"Anything you want, I'll do."

"Call a guy at LAPD, name's Sergeant Martinez, works on that airport bombing happened a while back. Tell him you're bringing in Mary Alice Baker." I hung up before he could ask what.

I stopped in a health food store, wanted a coke and ham sandwich, rabbit food was all they had. I bought a sprout sandwich and orange juice, walked back to my car. Peeled off my wet jeans, hung them over the ventilation duct, dried them out driving to the gallery. I parked in the street across the lot, ate, watched the rear entrance. Bobby Easter's Rolls was parked near the back door. While I was drinking the last of the juice, Billy b's pick up truck pulled into the lot. He hopped out of his truck, hustled into the building.

I had a gun, so why not do it? I stepped out of the car, jammed the revolver into my waist-band, zipped up the leather jacket so nobody could see I was carrying. I took the back stairs, rang the buzzer, waited. The door wedged open to Bobby Easter, looking surprised to see me.

I said, "I need to talk to Billy b."

"You just missed him."

I pulled the gun out of my pants, pointed it at his head. I said, "You don't let me in, I won't miss you, not this close."

He backed into the gallery. I slid inside, eased the door shut behind me. Easter held his hands up, started stuttering something sounded like, "Don't shoot." Surprised me how scared he looked. Maybe Billy b said I went crazy on him. Maybe it was just the gun.

I said, "You got a closet, someplace small?"

Easter pointed to a door behind the reception desk.

I backed around the desk, opened the door. Perfect. A closet filled with office supplies, a man-sized standing space. I crooked a finger at Easter, said, "Get in."

He looked at me like he didn't want to. I encouraged him with the barrel of my revolver. He didn't move. He said, "I . . . I . . . I . . . I . . ." Like he was some kind of stuck record. Fear can do that to somebody. I walked over, said, "You the one called the cops on me?"

He just stood there, stared at me, said, "I . . . I . . . I . . . I . . ."

"You don't have to speak. Just nod, up and down."

His chin dipped to his breastbone, bobbed back up. I pushed him into the closet. He didn't fight it, stood facing the shelves, hands still raised above his head. I wondered what I was supposed to do now, hit him on the back of the head, like I'd seen them do on television?

I said, "Be a good boy, stay quiet. If I hear this door open, I'll hurt you."

I closed the door, wedged the receptionist's chair under the handle, went to find Billy b. The gallery was big, ten thousand square feet at least. I followed the trail of Billy b's paintings. Sharon Stone and Billy Baldwin kissing, Arnold Schwarzenegger blowing something up, a super close-up of lips that had to be Kim Basinger's, an entire room devoted to Elvis paintings. In the last room, it was me up on the wall. The canvas was maybe ten feet high by fifteen feet long. The painting was a double portrait. On the left, I stood looking like a prom queen. Frilly pink dress, roses in my arms, blonde curls spilling below a golden crown. The right side, I had my dyed-black hair, carried an AK-47 assault rifle. Looked like I wanted to kill somebody.

I back-tracked to Elvis, saw a closed door, opened it to a small room where extra paintings, some ladders and paint supplies were stored. Billy b sat in the middle of the room, legs crossed half-lotus style, hands resting on his knees like he was meditating. Mounted on the wall in front of him, low to the ground and turned three-quarters profile, was the thing from the case. He didn't react to me coming up behind him, didn't turn his head, had this strange glow on his face.

I put the gun in my jacket pocket, squatted down in front of him, said, "I forgive you about that girl, but the other shit we gotta talk about."

Billy b said, "Do you have any idea how important this is?"

I said, "You called the police on me."

"It's the font, the source, everything Warhol did streams from this one work of art, everything Koons has thought of, everything I've painted."

"Easter just confessed, don't bother trying to lie."

He reached out, took my hand, pointed to the thing on the wall, he said, "Look at the shape, Nina, look at the flowing curve from top to bottom, doesn't it remind you of something?"

"Sure, it reminds me of a plumbing fixture."

"Think icon. Think Buddha. Think the Madonna."

It was useless trying to talk to him. I got up, found the black case behind some paintings, rolled it over to the thing. It was attached to the wall with hooks, lifted off easy.

Billy b said, "Wait a minute, I thought you *got* it."

I set the thing carefully down inside the case, said, "I got it alright, and now I'm taking it out of here."

He stepped between me and the exit, jumped out of the way when he saw I wasn't stopping, I'd run over him if I had to. He chased me through the door, shouting, "Don't you know anything about Art? Don't you know who Duchamp is?"

He ran around the other side of the case, put his arms out, stopped me from rolling it any more.

"You're angry, you have a right to your anger, but think about it for a second, it wasn't me, I didn't call the police. I wasn't ready yet, I needed to paint more celebrity criminals before you got arrested."

I felt angry and hard. I said, "You brought your paintings and the case here the day before the raid. Why?"

"I got an anonymous tip."

"Sure you did."

"I think it was that producer friend of Cass's, she thought you were going to be at the loft that morning, decided the timing was right without consulting anybody else. Those Hollywood types will screw you every time. The important thing is we're together again. We should call the police, turn ourselves in, Cass's producer friend is waiting for us to call, we can turn ourselves in live on television."

"You know her number?"

He reached for his t-shirt pocket, said, "Sure, I have it right here."

I pulled the revolver out of my jacket, pointed it at him, said, "You, Easter and this Wanker lady, you three put your little heads together, decided it was time to turn me in?"

Billy b looked at the gun like he was waiting for a punch line. I mean, we'd slept together and now I was holding a gun on him. He couldn't believe it. That was two guys in one day looked at me like that, ready to make the same mistake. He said, "Nina, you are acting seriously paranoid. This isn't the Twilight Zone. It's Santa Monica.

I said, "Move the case down to my car."

Billy b laughed at me like it was a big joke.

I said, "I'm not kidding."

"And if I don't, what are you going to do, shoot me?" He leveled his forefinger at me, said, "Bang! Got you first."

I sighted the revolver over his left shoulder and fired. Give him credit, he didn't flinch more than a little. When the reverberation died out, he glanced back to see where the bullet went. Crotch-center on a painting of Elvis in blue jeans and bare chest.

Billy b yelped like I'd shot him, said, "You shot Elvis!"

I sighted the gun and fired again and again, put holes waist-level in the two Elvises flanking the first. I said, "Fuck Elvis."

Shoot at a guy a couple times, he gets the point the relationship is over. No need to argue about anything, no point pretending you feel bad things didn't work out. Maybe Billy b saw I was truly dangerous. I wasn't his lover any more. Not even his friend. I was an angry woman with a gun. He rolled the case down, hoisted it onto the back-bed of the mini-truck.

I slammed the gate shut, said, "Nice knowin' ya."

Billy b backed toward the gallery, said something got lost in a squeal of tire-rubber. Always a lot of car noise in LA but this noise turned my head. A car was coming through the lot way past advisable speed. I knew the car, saw it before, sprinted for the wheel. A second Chevy was coming fast from the opposite direction. As quick as I could move wasn't quick enough. The first Chevy slid crosswise against the curb, the second pinned my back bumper. They were good, I didn't have two inches room to maneuver, but they shouldn't have tried working the same trick twice. I whipped the wheel to the curb, floored the accelerator, popped the clutch. The mini-truck lurched forward, half jumped the curb, smacked the fender of the front Chevy. I stood on the accelerator, let the motor roar and tires smoke. The Chevy inched sideways. I caught a flash of movement in the side mirror, the guy behind trying to sneak out the door. I switched the revolver to my left hand, reached blind out the window, ducked the guy down with a wild shot.

The front Chevy gave ground, looked like it was going to break free, then wedged against the curb and held. Tires blistered and smoked, the mini-truck went nowhere. The guy in front, it was Frack, I saw him slip out, sight his gun over the hood. I ducked under the wheel. The windshield cracked overhead. I jammed the transmission into reverse, kept the RPMs red-lined. The gears screamed and held. The mini-truck roared back, slammed the car behind. Gun and tire smoke bit my lungs. The windshield splintered a second time, glass bit into my face. I shifted into first and put my foot through the floor. The mini-truck rocketed forward. A couple feet of run-up was all it needed, those big tires jumped the curb and the front bumper hit the Chevy high. If I couldn't go around, I was going through or over it. The mini-truck climbed up the Chevy, pitched radically on its side, I was dead afraid I was going all the way over so I twisted the wheels straight and that did it. Sheet metal crunched and ripped. I popped my head above the door frame, saw Frack's mouth open astonished as the mini-truck clawed over the hood of his car. The rear tires cleared, the bumper gouged asphalt coming down, broke half off, dragged sparks. The mini-truck rocked and rolled. In the rearview I could see Frack sighting down his gun. I ducked low and whipped around the first corner. The bumper snapped, cartwheeled off. I didn't see anybody coming after me in the rearview. I laughed and cursed, seemed like I got away free.

Bullets were scattered loose in three different pockets

of Wrex's jacket. He always was the disorganized type, never could count on him putting things in order. I held onto the steering wheel with one hand, notched in the cartridges one by one. It only stood to reason the surviving Drake brother would show up at Bobby Easter's gallery, seeing as I blabbed all about it when they had a hold of me. I'd got lucky, with the help of a little skill and violence. I wasn't going to count on getting lucky twice. As long as the thing in the case was in open play, I couldn't count on a peaceful night's sleep. Jail was beginning to look like a real holiday compared to the way my life was going. At least in jail only the state would be trying to kill me. I drove like I was the only car on the road, weaving in and out of lanes, speeding through oncoming traffic when the road jammed up. I kept my eye on the rear-view, was sure nobody could follow, not the way I was driving.

I parked across the street from Ben's office, ran into the building. The office door was locked. I took out the key, opened the door. Ben was sitting in his chair. His eyes were closed. I thought he was sleeping. Then I saw what happened to him. I sat on the floor and cried. It didn't make any sense for them to do that. Not to Ben. Maybe they thought he knew something he didn't. Maybe he learned what was going on, tried to stop them. I don't know. Never will. I haven't cried since. That was the moment the hardness took me over. The small, nut-hard place I always retreated to was all I had left. The soft parts were sheared clean off when I saw the bullet hole in Ben's head.

I don't know how long I sat on the floor. Too long. I was still crying when I heard the stairs creak once, then again, somebody too heavy to be quiet. The only hiding place was a utility closet to the side of Ben's desk. I snuck inside, quietly latched the door shut.

Whoever entered the office wasn't surprised at seeing Ben. The door closed softly. I listened for footsteps, didn't hear any. I didn't hear anything at all, but I knew he was outside the door, I couldn't tell exactly where. I had the gun gripped in both hands, ready to shoot the moment I heard the first latch click. He had to know I was in there. The closet was the only place I could hide. If he knew where I was, he wouldn't have to touch the door-knob. He could shoot me dead as he wanted, right through the door. Just like I planned to do to him. I crouched low, waited for it to happen, anticipated exactly where the bullets would strike. I wondered how much it would hurt before the shock dulled the pain and death smothered it out. I wondered what was going to happen to me then. I'm not ashamed to say I told God I was sorry for all the bad things I'd done.

The smell of gasoline drifted up from the crack at the

bottom of the door, I saw it trickling dark and wet at my feet. A metallic click sounded somewhere out in the room. Seconds passed where I heard nothing, not even my fear-stopped heart. Sulfur flared out, a bright ripping sound. I knew that sound. Watched the bright flame meet the tip of a cigarette, the cigarette snuff out in my flesh.

I flicked the barrel of the gun toward the match-strike, fired twice through the door. Then it was like the air in the room was sucked out. Fire spurted under my feet. I kicked at the door, knew I'd been given the choice of burning or catching bullets as I ran. A bullet seemed faster. The door jerked open like a curtain to hell. I pulled the leather jacket over my head and dove, came up clear of fire. A shriek tore across the other side of the office. Frack ran at me, flames shooting from his skin. I shot him in the chest, slammed him to the ground. He lay there, twitching, hands mechanically trying to beat the flames from his face. I walked over, shot him again. The only thing moving about him then was the fire.

I backed into the corridor, ran halfway down the stairs, stopped and listened for the guy in the second car, didn't want to run into a bullet. Smoke billowed across the ceiling, down the stairwell. Couldn't breathe. Didn't have much choice, I burst out the front door in a thick cloud of smoke, rolled behind the fender of a parked car.

The second guy was idling his Chevy across the street.

I recognized the car easy by the bashed-in door. When he saw it was me running out, he took off. I stood up, surprised to see him run, noticed the gate of the minitruck pulled down. The bastard had the case. Let him run. The Chevy didn't have much of an engine. I was sure I could catch him. No way I was going to let him keep it. If they killed me like they killed Ben, so what. I started across the street, fished the keys from my pocket, stopped short. The front tire was slashed flat. I wasn't following anybody.

It didn't make me angry. Slashing my tire was the smart thing to do. I felt disappointed. I flipped open the cylinder, looked inside. I still had two bullets left. Wanted to use them. I searched the jacket for more, felt something metal I forgot about. The key to Wrex's bike. Parked one block away, corner of Sunset Boulevard.

The Harley was like riding a thundercloud. It made me feel strong. I let the Harley fly between lanes, braked sharply for turning cars, swerved into opposite traffic when lanes were blocked. I spotted the Chevy just inside Koreatown. Like I figured, the guy had chosen the shortest route to Fleischer's office. He was in a flock of cars one light change ahead of me. I slowed the bike, coasted between lanes to the head of the queue. When the light turned green, I gave the bike some throttle. The Chevy was in the right-hand lane. I swung into the lane three cars behind, followed it five blocks before the timing and situation looked right. He was driving fast but cautious, not dawdling but not taking any chances either. I wheeled the Harley into the center lane again, threaded the white line between lanes. Bikes take advantage of traffic like this all the time. Most normal thing in the world. The guy didn't even look at me until I was already there, gun out and pointing at his head. I knew him from the videotape. It was Mike Fleischer. I had no mercy in me. I shot him in the face.

Something so small as a bullet, it wasn't enough to kill a guy like Fleischer, take off half his jaw maybe, but not kill him. He jerked the wheel, tried to crush me against a car the next lane over. I lost it braking, nearly took a flying lesson over the handle-bars. The Chevy smacked into the car in the next lane, knocked it into oncoming traffic. I straightened out the bike, saw cars looked like blurs coming at me, everybody trying to get out of the way of the big stuff, a motorcycle like mine the best thing to hit if you've got to hit something. I closed my eyes, gave the bike full throttle, screamed through the panic weave of cars, came out the other side surprised.

Fleischer was hit, I knew I hit him, he was running fast, couldn't control the car at high speed. I didn't think about it, gripped the pistol in my left hand and swung the bike up the Chevy's right flank. The Chevy drifted side to side, I didn't know if Fleischer was trying to make himself harder to hit or if he was just losing it. I crouched low over the bike, sighted the gun on the back of his head. The light ahead turned red, I never got the chance to pull the trigger, Fleischer was going for it. I jammed the gun into my pocket, went too. A truck pulled out from the right when the Chevy's wheels hit the crossing. Big, bright yellow, a sixteen-wheeler. The Chevy went left, I went right, but the son-of-a-bitch was too big, I couldn't get around it, was going too fast to stop, I only had one choice. It was a kamikaze move, laying the bike down, no timing to it, just luck or death. I pushed away from the bike, took the pavement on the back of my leather jacket, slid under the carriage, saw those big wheels clamp down on Wrex's Harley, chew it to scrap. But the wheels didn't get me, I slid clear, came to a stop a couple feet the other side. It was all so fast and easy I thought I'd died, was dreaming it all up from the afterlife, thought maybe this is what happens in death, you don't feel a thing. I sat up, looked for my dead body, like you sometimes see in the movies when somebody dies. But there wasn't any dead part I could see, guessed that meant I was alive.

Lay a bike down in the middle of an intersection, you'd think somebody would get out of their car, see if you were okay, but every one was looking across the street, a big commotion was happening at the corner gas station. Fleischer's Chevy had come up against the pumping island, sheared one of the pumps off at the base. Gasoline gushed from the pump, flowed in a fat arc toward the street, the gas shimmered in the twilight like a rainbow. The pot at the end was one of those asphalt heating machines, guys on the next building over were doing a roofing job, they started shouting everybody away. I saw what was about to happen sure as thunder follows lightning, jumped to my feet, ran toward the Chevy. A drop of hot asphalt dripped down, touched the gas, the gas lit like a fuse, a gas station attendant saw me running, tackled me down when the whole thing went up in a fireball six stories high. Biggest noise I ever heard, made the bomb at the airport sound like a firecracker. Then came the sucking noise fire makes, some of the guys around started hooting and hollering, and I must admit, it was a pretty sight, if I wasn't seeing my whole future going up in flames I might have hooted too.

The gas station attendant, he had a name patch on his shirt read Kim, he let me off the ground, said, "You crazy, lady? You get yourself killed."

I think tears were still streaming down my face from Ben. I said, "Something in the car I had to get."

Kim asked, "You knew the guy in that car?"

I nodded.

"Forget it, he's cooked, nobody could survive that."

I said, "Good."

23

I knew it would look better if I turned myself in, didn't feel like it. I took a bus to the office. Fire-trucks parked up and down the street, the Ivar Theater gutted, nobody paid much attention as I changed the front tire on the mini-truck. I drove out to Venice Beach again, slept in the front seat.

I woke sometime after midnight, the sound of gunfire in my head, couldn't get back to sleep. I got out of the truck, walked the back streets and alleys. I could sense guys on the street watching me, thinking a young woman all alone here this time of night, easy target. But I wasn't afraid. It was a weird feeling, walking down bad streets in the dead of night, not being afraid. After all the times I was terrified some guy was going to come after me, of being a walking target because of what I got between my legs. It was the fear once bothered me most, the constant wondering if this was when the beast was going to roar out of the shadows to rip me up. I fantasized this would be the moment the beast came. I saw him spring from the alley darkness, I said, "You want a little of what I got?" Then I'd whip out the revolver, and after, his voice would come out a couple octaves higher, if it came out at all.

I walked back to the car, slept some more.

The next morning I bought a newspaper. The headline read

FALLING OUT IN TERRORIST GANG
THREE SHOT TO DEATH A FOURTH WOUNDED

The story didn't release any names but the wounded one had to be Wrex, the story said they arrested a suspect downtown with gunshot wounds. On page three was a drawing of my face. It was me down to my short black hair and nose stud. The only detail wrong about the drawing was the mouth, turned down like I wanted to kill somebody.

I searched out a drug store in a Hispanic neighborhood. Fewer people there to read the *Times*, recognize me. I bought scissors, a bottle of water, a razor blade, sunglasses, some shaving cream, a baseball cap. I drove back to the beach, laid everything out on the front seat, used the rearview mirror to guide me as I whacked away at my hair with the scissors. When I'd cut as close down as I could with the scissors, I lathered up the shaving cream, drew the razor across my skull. The crisp scrape of metal on virgin skin yielded to the cool tingle of air. I rinsed the razor and drew it across my skull again, traced the blade around the hidden curves, over the ridge where the spine connects to the brain. I leaned my head out the window to rinse off, felt my skull in my hands, bare and smooth as water-worn granite. The baseball cap was black with a big X on the front. I pulled it down over my eyes, checked it out in the mirror. It was cool. I looked like a boy.

I pulled my camera from behind the seat, thought maybe I'd shoot a self-portrait. The cool metal ridges of the focus ring felt like Braille under my fingers. I brought the viewfinder world up to my eye, suddenly saw things different. The frame limited and shaped, gave focus to things, crafted meaning where before there was confusion. I used film to remember what specific moments felt like in the crisp and distant reality of this other world. Most often, I photographed what I recognized as me, like walking through a strange house, searching for reassuring glances in every mirror along the way.

Wasn't hard figuring out where the guy who owned the mini-truck lived, Phil it was, his address was written on the registration in the glove box. I drove north, over the pass from Sylmar. On the road, I had to laugh, it was the girls who looked over, checked me out. Macho truck, wrap-around sunglasses, baseball cap over shaved head, the confident smile you get when you got a gun in your pocket, I must have looked pretty hot, must have given them a little thrill, knew I would have been thrilled a few weeks ago, seeing somebody like me.

I parked the mini-truck a block up, wrote a nice note to Phil, thanked him for loaning me his wheels, was sorry I had to return them dented up. When it got dark, I took the note and the keys to the address on the registration, dropped them both in the mail box. Then I walked through town. Even when I was small it never seemed like a very big town, I could always walk from one side to the other in an hour. I passed the park, saw kids in the shadows under the trees, smoking dope and drinking beer, watching out for cops. I walked down Main Street, not much happening that time of night, a couple guys sitting in a parking lot brown-bagging beers, a jacked-up Ford cruising up one way then down the other, looking for action. I crossed the street I grew up on, pulled the revolver from my jacket, jammed it between my belt and belly, then I walked down the street, smelled the trees, the grass, the rich automobile perfume always in the air, the mix of gas, oil, rust.

The house looked just like I remembered from the lifetime ago I'd last seen it. A GI-loan house from the fifties. One story. Wood-frame. Tarpaper roof. Oil stains on the driveway. Lawn fading to brown, no matter what the season. I closed my eyes, remembered the interior. The brown coffee table chipped at the corner where my sister Sharon hit her head getting knocked down. The dent in the hallway, where my brother George slammed his fist because he couldn't bring himself to hit back. The scrubbed-out spots of blood in the corner of the family room, where I crouched the day I took six stitches in my mouth. I had one bullet left, centered in the firing chamber. The porch light was on. Even a bad home sometimes looks good coming back to it.

I figured the guy slumped in the front seat of the brown sedan parked down the street was FBI surveillance. I knocked on the window to wake him, slouched up the walkway to the front door, took out my key and opened it. The living room was empty, dark. A wedge of light came from the kitchen, angled across the far wall. Everybody was in there having dinner, I could hear the wordless clank of knives and forks. I walked through the dark, past the living room into the light.

Pop sat at the far end of the table, he saw me first, was spooning down his soup when I came in, the sight froze the spoon to his lips. Next chair over, Ray sucked in a lung-full of air. Mom turned in her chair, cried out, at first I thought because she was afraid, didn't recognize me, but she jumped up, ran at me with her arms out. I nearly knocked her over I hugged her so hard. Nothing was going to stop her from crying, and there was something about seeing my mom cry almost made me cry too. Maybe I would have cried, if I had a little more time to work up to it. Maybe not. Maybe I was a little dead inside. I didn't get much time to try.

Pop stood up at the far end of the table, said, "What're you doing here?"

Mom's arms went stiff around my neck.

Pop said, "Stand away, she's not our daughter anymore."

Mom said I hadn't meant any harm.

Pop yelled, "Stand away!"

Mom jumped. She didn't want to, but she did. She moved to Ray. Ray put his arm around her, watched Pop.

Pop said, "If you ever show up here again, I'll break your neck."

I knew then where I got my anger. I knew how it was possible for me to kill people. I got it from him. He gave it to me with my bones, my teeth, my ligaments and joints. It was encoded in the DNA at the moment of my conception.

I said, "I didn't come to see you. I came to see Mom."

I saw it happening to him. The beast coming out. It didn't take much time. One second. Maybe two. Coil and spring. He came across the linoleum, cocked his fist and

292

roared, "Get out of this house before I kill you! Get out of the goddamn . . ."

I jerked the gun out, stuck it in his face before he could finish the sentence. It stopped him cold.

I said, "Have a chair, Pop."

I saw him thinking. Thinking too much. About whether I had the guts to actually shoot him. I cocked back the hammer. Motive. Opportunity. Weapon. Guts. I had them all. I said, "At the table. Like you usually do. Chair turned around backwards. We'll sit around the kitchen table, just like regular family."

He knew I'd shoot him. He wasn't a coward, I'll give him that. He wasn't afraid. But he knew. He backed up to his chair, turned it around, sat down. Mom and Ray, they took their places at the table. Ray's eyes were on the gun, Mom's eyes on my face.

I said, "You thirsty, Pop? Of course you're thirsty. You're always thirsty." I opened the refrigerator door, tossed him a beer. "Have a beer. Have several beers. Get stinking drunk. Get piss-stinking angry drunk. Get so drunk you forget I have a gun."

He set the bottle on the table, said, "You made your point, Mary."

I put the gun to his head. The rage shot through my nerves so hot and strong my hand shook. "I said drink."

He broke the seal on the beer, took a long swig.

"How can you say I'm not your daughter?"

Mom said, "He didn't mean it that way, honey."

Pop said, "Goddamn it, of course I meant it. Don't *you* tell me what I mean or not."

I came perilous close to shooting him then.

Ray knew it, said, "Mary."

"What?"

"Put the gun down, okay?"

I didn't put the gun down, I said, "Tell me why I'm not your daughter."

The gun barrel pressed against the bone behind his ear. If I shot him, the bullet wouldn't penetrate his skull, alter his convictions at all. The bullet would bounce off, no harm done. His head was harder than steel plate. Everything about the man was hard.

He said, "I did the best I could with you, but you stopped being mine. I got no idea who you are, and I don't care."

"You disown me?"

"That's right."

I showed him the gun, barrel first.

"I shot three men. I thought about you coming after me with your big hands and I shot two of them dead. I thought about all the times you hit me and Mom, and the anger came up so hot and hard I knew it had to come from you. Only my fists aren't as big as yours and I can't hit as hard. So I got a gun. I got a gun but it was your finger helped me pull the trigger."

He said, "I raised you the best I could."

"You didn't raise me. You stunted me."

The phone rang. We let it ring.

I said, "Get out of the house. Get out of the house before I get angry again. I don't want to shoot you. If I shot you, I'd have to shoot myself after, and I've only got one bullet left."

He looked at me like I was kidding him, there was no way I could order him out of his own house. I pointed to the back door, I roared, "Get out of the goddamn house!"

He edged away from the table, unlocked the back door. He didn't want to walk straight out of the house like I ordered him. Walking out was too much like turning tail. He said, "I did those things because, well, because that was me. Just like you do the things you do because that's you. You throw all your sins at my feet, I'll just kick 'em away. Your sins are yours."

Then he walked out the door, didn't bother to close it behind him. Typical. I walked over, slammed it shut. The phone was still ringing. I told Mom to answer it.

She picked up the phone, said, "Yes, yes it is. Just a moment." Mom cupped the phone in the palm of her hand, whispered, "It's the FBI honey. Do you wanna talk?"

I grabbed the phone. The guy on the other end of the line seemed nice enough. I think he was anxious it might be a hostage situation, asked if I was carrying any weapons. I told him of course I was carrying weapons, what kind of dangerous criminal would I be if I wasn't even carrying a gun? It would be a waste of media space and FBI time if I didn't have at least a pistol on me. If I didn't have any weapons, they could send the meter maid to arrest me, and that would make everybody look kind of silly, now wouldn't it? California's most dangerous criminal apprehended by off-duty meter maid. The news ratings would fall, the advertisers wouldn't be happy, nobody would go out and buy extra newspapers, what an anticlimax, I couldn't afford to disappoint the public like that.

I suspect the FBI agent thought I was a little crazy. He told me to calm down, everything could be worked out, the last thing he wanted was for anybody to get hurt, including me. I laughed at him. I said he was too late. He should have come by here twenty years ago if he wanted to stop people from getting hurt. Then I hung up the phone.

Mom put on a brave face, said, "So. You're in a little trouble."

"Sure am."

"Don't worry, honey, we'll get the best lawyers."

"You can't afford it, Mom. You don't have any money."

"We'll sell the house."

"Over Pop's dead body."

"Don't be so hard on your Pop. Life's been tough for him, you know."

"Tougher than for everybody else? Tougher than for you? So tough he's gotta beat the hell out of you or anybody he can get his hands on when he gets mad? That tough? And what the hell's wrong with you that you stay with him? Are you sick in the head? Are you so weak you'll suffer any pain, take any abuse, just so you won't have to live alone?"

Mom's eyes were shining blanks. This is the look she always gets when the talk is about something she doesn't know how to handle. Mom lived with the guy forty years. I sometimes think the beaten and broken value loyalty because nothing else glues them together.

Mom said, "We can talk about this some other time?"

"I want to talk about it now!"

Ray said, "Mary, please, give me the gun."

I glanced down at my hand, saw the barrel pointed toward my mom.

I said, "I'm sorry. Things are just a little tense for me right now."

I set the safety, dropped the pistol onto the table. Then

I sat down, stared off into space, wanted to cry but couldn't come close, was too hard and dry inside. Ray shoved the pistol to the far side of the table, asked if I wanted a beer, got us all one. The heavy clatter of helicopter blades flew over the house, turned a wide circle, flew over again. A bright light beamed into the back yard. The sound of a helicopter, that's always scared me. A helicopter overhead, it's looking for somebody, and if it's you, there's no escaping it. Can't outrun a helicopter.

Ray opened three beers; handed one to Mom, one to me. We drank. I could hear the machinery of law and order out on the street. Motors, car doors, voices. Mom reached out, held my hand. The helicopter flew in circles, around and around the house, the searchlight swept the back yard corner to corner. Looked like a spotlight, waiting for somebody to step into it. I heard a gate close, sudden and sharp, knew time was about out.

I said, "Take care of Mom, Ray."

I stood, gave him a kiss, embarrassed him. Except for me and Mom, we weren't a kissing family.

She said, "Do you want me to go with you?"

I said, "No, Mom."

She said, "I'm not . . ." Then stopped.

I looked at her, waited, asked, "What is it?"

"It's not dying I'm scared of."

I smiled, kissed her cheek. She knew I understood. I walked to the front door, opened it, stepped onto the front porch.

They didn't expect me to just walk out like that, not a dangerous renegade like me. There were over a hundred of them out there. Sheriff cars lined both sides of the street. Each car had two Sheriffs, each Sheriff had a gun, minimum two pistols, one shotgun per car. Some guys in blue suits, they had guns too, stood behind brown cars. Everybody with a gun had it pointed at me. I heard clicks go up and down the line, the sound of bullets being chambered. At the far end of the street, a fire truck, an ambulance, four or five vans. The vans were all marked with call letters and slogans, had people running over with cameras, microphones.

Overhead, the helicopter flew around and around. The searchlight danced over the roof, the front yard, and then I was in it, spotlights came on from twenty cop cars, I was lit from above, the sides, dead ahead. White, searing light. The light scorched, blinded me. I put my hands to my eyes, stumbled down the steps.

A voice came out of a bullhorn, a voice stern and commanding, the tone of the voice said don't fuck around, do what we tell you. The voice said, "Put your hands behind your head, kneel to the ground."

I put my hands up, didn't want them to think I had a

gun, was going to shoot all one hundred of them, but I wasn't going to kneel for anybody.

The voice said, "Kneel down, kneel to the ground."

I said, "Go ahead and shoot, but I'm not kneeling."

The voice said, "This is your last warning. Kneel to the ground."

I turned my hands around in the air, gave them the finger, said, "Fuck you."

The voice couldn't think what to say next, nobody seemed willing to shoot me, at least not live on television. I saw six of them coming at me out of the lights, six guns sighted down on my chest, the cops moved like cops do when they're making an arrest of a dangerous suspect, inching forward one step at a time, the way the light hit them from behind, they looked like angry beings from another planet. When they got close, two of the cops circled to the side, kept out of each other's line of fire. The cop most in front, his face stretched back so I could see his teeth, he barked, "Kneel to the ground!"

I said, "Never."

I wound up flat on my face a second later, a boot on my neck, my arms yanked back and wrists nylon-cuffed together. People who watched the news that night say it was the strangest thing, I was smiling when the cops pulled me up, and when they led me past the news crews, the lights and cameras, I gave a bigger smile, made me look like I was either crazy or a wannabe movie star.

It wasn't that at all. Maybe I had just been arrested and was going off to jail for a hundred hard years, maybe I had just lost everything a normal person values in life, but I didn't do what they told me. They didn't break me, that made me the freest person on earth.

I'm in County Jail now. Seems during what the newspapers call my two-week crime spree, I broke half the
criminal code. The district attorney couldn't make up his
mind where to start there were so many things he could
charge me with. Murder one, murder two, manslaughter,
multiple counts of assault with a deadly weapon, grand
theft, unlawful discharge of a firearm, unlawful pos-
session of explosive materials, not to mention two unpaid
parking tickets and driving a motor vehicle without a
valid license. The prosecutor claims I'm the worst night-
mare a society can have. A rogue feminist killer. I have a
history of hating men, beginning with my father. It seems
Lizzie Borden was a saint compared to me.

I never expected to get out of all this with a stern
lecture and a slap on the wrist. Wrex cut a deal with the
DA, looks like he's going to skate on all charges. According to him, it was me who knew the Drake brothers. He
was a pitiful figure in court, crutched up to the witness
stand, right leg in a cast. Even cut his hair, wore a suit.

Under oath, he admitted it was his gun shot the older Drake dead, but his version of events that night is considerably different than mine. He claimed I double-crossed the Drake brothers, and in retaliation they kidnapped me. Wrex was following the Drakes, because he knew they were bad hombres. It was his bet they'd track me down, hurt me when they did, maybe even kill me. The prosecutor asked him why he went to all that trouble on my account. In front of judge, jury and world press Wrex sobbed, "God forgive me, but I still love her."

How I wished then for just one more bullet!

Under expert guidance from the prosecutor, Wrex said he waited outside the house until one Drake left, then broke in, got the drop on the other. The situation was tense, he said, but no sir, he didn't shoot nobody. He had to make a phone call to set me up with a safe place to stay for the night. He wanted to take Frick out to the phone with him, but I told him to give me the gun, I'd watch Frick while he was gone. Wrex had just picked up the phone when he heard first one shot, then another. Frick was dead on the floor when he ran back to see what happened. Then he saw me pump three bullets into Frick's dead body.

"And what was the defendant's reaction?" the prosecutor asked, his voice gentle, as though poor Wrex's nervous system couldn't take the excitement.

"I asked her, you know, like what happened, did he go for the gun or something? The look on her face, that's Mary's face, the defendant's face I mean, well, it was kinda crazy. All she said was, and please excuse me for using a cuss word, but I'm repeating what she said, which was, 'Rest in pieces, asshole.'"

That's murder one in the DA's book. With both Drake brothers dead, no way I could prove Wrex wrong. My prints were on the gun, my paraffin test positive. Wrex testified I shot him in the leg out of pure meanness, then ran him over with his own bike. I went on to kill the other Drake brother, gun down Mike Fleischer and threaten to put a bullet through my own father, establishing what the prosecutor called a pattern of wanton homicidal behavior. This isn't even counting the charges against me for terrorism, murder and mayhem in the airport bombing. So far, the only shooting I haven't been charged with is Elvis's. I'm sure I'll hear from his lawyers before this is through.

Nobody believes my story about what I found inside the case, nothing was left after the gas station explosion to prove or disprove anything. Billy b and Bobby Easter have kept their mouths shut on the advice of their lawyers. The prosecution theorizes Kabyenko was smuggling heroin into the country, hidden in Russian plumbing supplies. Half the trial, I waited for my lawyer to present the letters Kabyenko wrote to Fleischer, and the videotape Cass and I shot of Fleischer in his office and the Drake brothers on the street. Was sure it all would prove my innocence, until the prosecutor got up, played the tape again, showed how I set up a deal with Fleischer, pointed to the paper bag of cash I traded for the case, said what we were seeing was obvious. A simple case of drug smuggling and murder for profit, gone terribly wrong. I could see how someone might see it that way, based on looking at the tape alone, felt pretty stupid after that. The letters he discounted as forgeries. Cass took the stand to testify to what she saw, told everybody the tape was a trick we were playing to prove my innocence, admitted she didn't see what was in the case, then she started talking about government conspiracies to support the cocaine and heroin cartels, didn't end up too credible.

All in all, jail isn't so bad. I have time to read. After fourteen years of school, I feel I'm finally getting an education. I get visitors. Mom comes once a week, sometimes with Ray. Rachel came once to talk about Ben. Cass comes to visit every now and then. The studio never hired her to write the script of my life story, big surprise, now she wants to make a documentary of me in jail, is pestering half the officials in the county trying to get permission. Some art professor came to see me, my lawyer sent him as part of my defense strategy. When

I told him what was in the case, he said I was lying or crazy or both, such a thing wasn't possible and he'd testify to that in court. My lawyer says there's no use trying to prove something you can't prove, advises me to keep my mouth shut about it.

Jerry hasn't bothered to come see me. Not that I blame him. Must have been a shock, learning who I was, what happened to Ben. I heard he's still in town, doing surveillance work nights, looking for missing persons days. I decided he had nothing to do with selling me out to the Drake brothers. Easier to sleep that way. Billy b did a couple interviews, some cable-access television, saw his name a couple times in stories written about me. Nobody asks him about his painting. They ask about me. The LACE exhibit sold every photo I printed. A couple art magazines ran profiles on me and my work. *Time* and *Newsweek* printed some of my photographs as part of their coverage. *Interview* sent somebody to ask about the differences between shooting 35 millimeter film and .38 caliber bullets. All three networks are doing movies of the week based on my story. Every other day somebody is on television talking about me. I got women's groups talking about how I'm a product of an abusive father. I got men's rights activists calling me a gun-slinging whore. I tell anybody who asks I'm just an average girl from a small California town who took a slightly wrong turn in life, is all. Nothing special about me, except circumstance, and circumstance can happen to anybody.

The trial is in its third month now. I've been in jail for over a year. My hair has grown out, but I keep it clipped short. After a big fight with my lawyer, I removed the dagger nose stud and skull earrings. I wear dresses to court. My lawyer, he said jurors are more likely to trust a blonde than a woman with black hair, so my hair is back to its original color. I even wear pink lipstick. I look like a good girl, again. But I know different.

Next week, my lawyer wants me to take the stand. He says the government doesn't have a good case against me for the Drake killings, but they're still waiting to file charges on Fleischer's death. My lawyer wants me to plead to manslaughter on that one. I showed him this story I'm telling you, let him read each chapter after I finished it. We talked about everything in here as part of the defense, but the trial never seems to get around to the why of things so much as arguing about the what. I've asked him a couple dozen times couldn't we copy this off and have the jury read it, let them decide from my own mouth whether I'm guilty or not. Every time I ask him he laughs and says the pure truth is like pure alcohol. Fatal in large doses, best to water it down a little.

Life isn't so bad. What I wanted most was a new life. I got it. They won't let me have a camera, but I guess I have to suffer somehow for my sins. I stay busy. I can't get into too much trouble. I don't have to worry about repeating the same self-destructive patterns. The state authorities have assumed responsibility for me.

I wish them luck.